Book Two of *The Methuselah Chronicles*

# The First Prophet

A Novel

by

## Terry Lee Hamilton

Foreword by

**Dr. John D. Morris**

**President, Institute of Creation Research**

*Dedicated to the memory of*
*my daughter, Glory (1984-1998).*

All scripture quotations are from the
King James Version of the Bible.



**First Edition**

Library of Congress
Catalog Card Number : 97-77036
ISBN 0-9660753-1-5

Published by
Glory to Glory Ministries
1813 E. 45th St.
Ashtabula, OH 44004
e-mail: hamiltonfamily@alltel.net
www.glorytogloryministries.com

# Table of Contents

**Table of Contents continued . . .**

# Foreword

The Bible gives us precious little in the way of details describing the fascinating pre-Flood times. We know that individuals lived to great ages. We also know that they were able to work metal, enjoyed music and poetry, and employed both agriculture and animal husbandry. Some lived in cities, some were pastoral.

All of the families we are told of had at least five children, with the age of the father ranging from sixty to five hundred. Perhaps the population grew rapidly. Some even had more than one wife.

The descriptions of the climate and hydrologic cycle reveal a world rather different from ours, and exceedingly favorable to life. We can learn from the fossil record of its plants and animals, that it was generally warmer with conditions supporting lush vegetation. Water was abundant and storms were essentially nonexistent. The ground was fertile and probably yielded its increase with minimal difficulty.

But this was not Eden. Adam and Eve had been banished from the Garden when they rebelled against God's authority. An angel guarded its entrance, forbidding any return. Without direct contact with the Creator, mankind soon degenerated into gross immorality. Murders followed, so did abandonment of the marriage covenant. Individuals were totally interested in selfish gain and wanton pleasure. Violence reigned throughout the Earth.

Some retained a knowledge of God, as seen by names chosen for their children, but only a small minority are said to have followed Him, and preached of Him to others. When judgment finally came, only eight true believers were left.

And so, that civilization is gone. Nearly all traces of it perished in the Flood waters. Only Noah and his immediate family accepted God's gracious gift of safety and lived to repopulate the world.

Who were these people, really? They must have been fascinating, highly capable individuals. Perhaps they were brilliant intellects, with strong bodies and good minds. Certainly their centuries of growth and health resulted in continued learning. Only in our recent technological age could modern engineers duplicate a ship the size of Noah's Ark, or even the monumental accomplishments of Noah's early post-Flood descendants.

They were people, just like us, or nearly so. They had marriage problems, injuries, rebellious kids, and business reversals. They had heartache and disease and disappointments. But they also knew joy and love and success.

How can we know them better? We can't, at least in this life. All we can do is imagine, moderating our imagination by the constraints of Scripture.

Or we can read *The Methuselah Chronicles*, written by Terry Lee Hamilton. His stories of Methuselah, his kin, and their experiences are fascinating and will carry your imagination along. Things may have happened just this way. We can appreciate not only Mr. Hamilton's imagination, but also his storytelling ability. I especially appreciate the way Scriptural concepts are interwoven into the story. Mr. Hamilton uses the very words of Scripture to teach truth.

* * * * * * * *

As I write this Foreword, I have only read the first two books of the seven-book series of *The Methuselah Chronicles*. I read them to my kids, and they loved them as much as I. All of us are waiting for the succeeding volumes. We want to know -- What happened to Crista?

***Dr. John D. Morris, President***
***Institute of Creation Research***

# Preface

Ever since ***Methuselah's Father*** was published in 1997, dozens and dozens of readers have asked me when Book Two of ***The Methuselah Chronicles*** was going to be published. After all, in the Foreword to ***Methuselah's Father***, Dr. John D. Morris, President, Institute of Creation Research, mentioned that he had already read a draft of Book Two. Please forgive me for making you wait so long and allow me this opportunity to explain the delay in publishing Book Two.

## Explanation for Delay of Publication

After ***Methuselah's Father*** was published in 1997, we had every expectation of publishing ***The First Prophet*** in 1998. However, God had another plan.

On June 23, 1998, during a family vacation in Georgia, our three children were in a tragic accident with an 18-wheel dump truck at a dangerous intersection. Our daughter Joy (then 20) and our son Daniel (then 17) miraculously survived, but God had another plan for our Glory. In the words of her pastor:

> Then there was Glory . . . whose 13-year-old body did not survive the terrible impact. She had to keep an appointment with Jesus. The Glory whom we all love so much, so full of life and love and music . . . a fine, Godly, sold-out young lady . . . went home to be with Jesus.

God used Glory in a mighty way during her thirteen years on Earth. Glory was one of the most active members and soulwinners at Lighthouse Baptist Church. An award-winning singer and pianist, Glory was the voice of Susie on our Boot the Mule musical adventure tapes. She had already started writing Christian songs and had the goal of being a Christian singer and writer.

But God had another plan. The grief which our family and church has borne has been boundless, but I can honestly say that I have not lost a daughter; I know right where she is. Shortly before her seemingly untimely death, Glory wrote the following words in her diary:

> I wonder if I'll have a long life. Like the verse in James, life is like a vapor, quickly gone. At least if I would die, I know I'm saved and going to Heaven to be with Jesus.

Glory! As Pastor Jones said, Glory was "full of life and love and music." She still is!

I can now better understand the grief and sorrow which I described in ***Methuselah's Father*** when Enoch lost his daughter Crista. Just as God promised Enoch that he would be reunited with Crista, God has given all of us Hamiltons the blessed promise that we will see Glory again. If you have trusted in Jesus as your Savior, then you will see Glory in Heaven, too!

## Explanation of the Title: *The First Prophet*

Please also allow me this opportunity to explain a potential controversy with regard to the title of Book Two. I have chosen, for literary purposes, the title ***The First Prophet***, although I am aware of the two Biblical passages (Matthew 23:34-35; Luke 11:49-51) which support the argument that Abel was the first prophet. I take nothing away from righteous Abel, who "being dead yet speaketh" (Hebrews 11:4). Abel's ministry was necessarily limited to his family; it would be neither unBiblical nor illogical to infer that God intended fathers to teach the Words of God "diligently unto thy children" (Deuteronomy 6:7).

Likewise, it would be neither unBiblical nor illogical to infer that, as time went on, many fathers failed in their duty to teach the Words of God to their children, resulting in a world in which "God saw that the wickedness of man was great in the earth" (Genesis 6:5).

Into such a wicked world, we are introduced to Enoch, the first prophet whose words and prophecies are recorded in Holy Scripture, as follows:

> And Enoch also, the seventh from Adam, prophesied of these, saying, Behold, the Lord cometh with ten thousands of his saints, To execute judgment upon all, and to convince all that are ungodly among them of all their ungodly deeds which they have ungodly committed, and of all their hard speeches which ungodly sinners have spoken against him.
> [Jude 14-15]

That's some powerful preaching . . . and prophesying! While Abel necessarily had a limited audience of three persons, Enoch on the other hand had an audience of untold numbers, preaching hard against sin in a very wicked world, yet prophesying a sublime message of hope to all succeeding generations that "the Lord cometh with ten thousands of his saints." The world needed a prophet such as Enoch back then; and the world needs prophets such as Enoch today. When Jesus does come back with ten thousands of His saints, Enoch will be in that crowd . . . and so will Methuselah . . . Noah . . . and Glory!

---

One final note: As much as I love ***Methuselah's Father***, I honestly believe that ***The First Prophet*** is even better. Let me know what your opinion is. God bless you!

# Prologue

## 1651 A.C.

The rhythmic chattering of the ancient staff alternated with the soft shuffling of ancient feet as the man hobbled across the hardwood floor toward the oaken desk at the far end of the room. Halfway across the room, the man paused, shifting his weight slightly against the unyielding strength and steadiness of the staff of God. In the early morning just before the dawn, his gaze shifted upward, through the window above the desk, focusing on the solitary brilliance of the bright and morning star.

The old man's chest was heaving, gasping for breath, whether from physical exertion or emotional release, no man, only God, could tell. Speaking only to himself and to his God, the gruff old man in his gruff old voice murmured his first words of the new day, "Nobody knows what it's like being nine hundred and sixty-five years old."

With another deep breath, the ancient one continued his journey to the far end of the room, fixing his gaze and attention on his destination -- the lambswool cushion on the seat of his favorite chair -- his writing chair, in front of his favorite desk -- his writing desk. Methuselah had seen neither of his inanimate friends for nearly a month, ever since that afternoon when Noah found him slumped over the desk, unconscious. "Humph," he thought to himself, "they didn't have to make such a fuss over me. It was only a little heart attack." Yet, Noah and his wife and all the others insisted that Methuselah take to bed and stay there until his strength returned.

Methuselah was not a good patient. "Let me out of bed!" he yelled every day. "Let me get back to my desk!" But someone stayed with him every minute, at least for the first three weeks. He wouldn't admit it, but the ancient one secretly relished all of the extra attention, all of the meals brought to him in bed. Nonetheless, he made life miserable for his nurses, demanding this and demanding that, until one of the ladies of the house happened upon a quiet idea. "Let's just ask Great-Grandpa to tell us some more of his stories about Enoch."

In the last year, Methuselah had grown to love to tell the stories about his father and mother and sister and Lamech and Noah and all the other incredible characters in Enoch's family. Methuselah could only chuckle at the memory of how resistant he had initially been to putting these family stories down on parchment. "I was a pretty stubborn old goat last year," he smiled to himself, "a lot like Adam's goat Obstinate."

As he made his way slowly across the room, Methuselah could tell that his breathing was much more labored than before. "Maybe this heart attack did take a little out of me," he wondered. "Well, don't they know that God isn't going to take me yet? I've got to finish writing the books."

His mind went back to that day one year ago when he started writing the first book. "I can't believe it took almost a year!" he mumbled to himself. "At this rate, I'll be six feet under before I finish the last book."

When he finally reached his writing chair, the ancient one collapsed, breathing great gulps of air. "I hope they don't find me for a few minutes," he said to himself. "I don't want them to see me like this." After a few minutes of quiet breathing, Methuselah let his mind wander back over the centuries, back to the time when his father was first saved, back when God called him to the office of prophet. "Father sure was strange at first," the old man recollected. "But what mighty miracles God wrought that first year!" Without another thought, Methuselah's hand reached over to his favorite quill, which he automatically dipped in his favorite ink bowl. Before anyone could stop him, Methuselah started writing the second book of ***The Methuselah Chronicles.***

# Part One

# Enoch's First Journey

**700 A.C.**

## Chapter One

# Homeward Bound

"Mom, do you think we will ever see Dad again?" asked Methuselah.

Her son's words startled Sarah out of her reverie. For hours they had sat in silence while their ox plodded his way from her father's home to the City of Gom. Sarah's mind had been many miles and many years away, dreaming of her home and her beloved husband Enoch, wondering if she would ever see him again.

"Mom, did you hear me?"

"What's that, son? What did you say?"

Now it was Methuselah's turn to wonder. For days, his mother had gaily chattered to him about her family and her childhood adventures growing up on Grandpa Meshach's farm. Methuselah hugely enjoyed and secretly envied his mother's stories of planting and harvesting, of working side by side with so many brothers and sisters. Methuselah had only one sister, and she was . . . she was . . . he hated to imagine where Crista, kidnapped and sold into slavery, might have been.

During their days of traveling, Methuselah noticed that his mother had never mentioned Enoch. By contrast, Methuselah's mind never strayed far from thoughts of his father, on a journey in search of God. Surely, thought Methuselah, Mom wondered what had happened to Dad. Why didn't she ever talk about him? Methuselah was expressing his darkest fear when he repeated, "Mom, do you think we will ever see Dad again?"

By now, Sarah had fully recovered her senses. She looked into her son's brown eyes and saw anguish and fear. Realizing that her son harbored the same dark thoughts that she had carefully concealed with happy chatter on their journey home, Sarah silently prayed, "Dear God, how can I encourage my son?"

Then, Sarah knew what to say. "Methuselah, without God's promises, we would be fearful of the future. I am trusting in God, not Enoch, to bring your father home to us."

Methuselah grimaced. "I thought you might bring God into this, Mom."

"Of course, son. God should be in everything we do. Although we have never seen Him face to face, we know Him by faith."

"Then why did Dad leave us to search for God?" the lad sensibly asked. "Couldn't Dad have found God by faith in our home?"

Sarah sighed. "Yes, he could have. But I truly believe that God is leading Enoch to Him in a very special way, and that God will someday soon lead Enoch home to us." Although she could sense that her son was not satisfied, mother and son sank back into silence as the ox slowly pulled their wagon along the road toward the City of Gom. Just before sunset of their ninth day on the road, Methuselah steered the ox through the north gate of the City of Gom. Heading in the direction of Ludim's blacksmith shop, Methuselah was fearful of finding Ludim home and having to endure one of his giant bearhugs; but he was even more fearful of not finding Ludim home and missing his friendly face. As God would have it, Ludim was just closing up shop when he saw the wagon and weary travelers. After gawking for a moment, Ludim rushed over, grabbed Methuselah out of the wagon, gave him a big bearhug, and guffawed, "Glory be! Perna will be glad to see you two travelers. Go on inside while I unhitch the wagon."

Just then, Perna came rushing out the back door. "You two must be famished. Go on inside and wash up and rest while I put dinner on." Soon, Methuselah was gulping down his first hot meal in over a week, ignoring the chatter of the three excited adults. Between sips of delicious lentil soup, Sarah shared the sad story of Enoch's visit to Jared's home. Ludim was especially grieved that his old friend Jared still had the form of religion but denied the power thereof.

Ludim's eyes brightened, however, as Sarah told of the visit to her parents' home. "Sarah," Ludim mused, "I only met your father one time at your wedding, but I could tell immediately that he was a righteous man, a believer in the One True God." Ludim looked Heavenward and exclaimed, "Lord, we need more men like Meshach on Earth today."

Ludim could not wait any longer to hear about Enoch and peppered her with questions. Sarah was relieved to tell the whole story again to her close friends about how her father had encouraged Enoch to search for Adam, but she tearfully confessed that she was concerned for Enoch's safety. Perna interrupted her friend sweetly, asking Ludim, "Honey, why don't we just stop eating for a minute and pray for Enoch's safety?" Upon hearing her words, Methuselah shoveled another hot biscuit in his mouth, reluctantly bowing his head as Ludim began to pray: "Lord, we thank You for safely returning Sarah and Methuselah to us. Please watch over dear Enoch as he searches for You. Lead him away from temptation, O Lord, and deliver him from the Evil One. And Lord, we beseech You to save Enoch's soul. Turn him toward You and make him a mighty voice here in the City of Gom. Until the Redeemer comes, Amen!"

# Chapter Two

# Homecoming

After dinner, Perna directed Sarah and Methuselah towards Tubal's old bedroom. "You two get a good night's rest. In the morning, you can head on home." As Perna retired, she stopped, turned back toward Sarah, and said, "By the way, Ludim and I drove out to your homestead a couple of times while you were gone to check on everything. Elihu is doing a fine job of keeping your house in order and watching the sheep." At the sound of Elihu's name, Methuselah became excited about seeing his good friend. But all excitement soon faded into a deep sleep for the weary travelers.

After a late breakfast, Ludim hitched the ox to the wagon, and soon Sarah and Methuselah were on their way home. Around lunchtime, they reached the top of the hill with the tamarisk grove overlooking the homestead. Sarah's heart fluttered as she looked down on her beautiful home. The sheepcote off to the right of the house was filled with fat sheep. The orchard and garden off to the left were lusciously green, filled with tempting fresh fruit and vegetables. As the wagon descended the dogwood-lined road to the house, Sarah noticed the thin wisp of smoke ascending from the courtyard. "My, my," she thought out loud, "Elihu is making our lunch."

Just then, the ox bellowed, and in a few seconds, the front door opened as Elihu looked up the hill to see who the company was. Methuselah blurted out his friend's name and watched as Elihu dashed up the hill, smiling widely and waving, exclaiming over and over, "You're home! You're home!"

Methuselah jumped down from the slowing wagon, slapped his friend on the back, and asked expectantly, "Did you miss me, Elihu?"

"I sure did, Methuselah, but I sorely missed your mother's cooking even more." Laughing as she watched the two boys run down the hill toward the sheepcote, Sarah grabbed the reins and led the ox down the hill to the front door of the house. Elihu, suddenly remembering his manners, rushed over to the wagon and assisted Sarah down from the wagon. "Welcome home, Miss Sarah," he shyly said. She gave the timid lad a brief hug and tenderly replied, "God bless you, Elihu. If you two boys unhitch the wagon, I will gladly finish lunch."

Sarah cautiously peeked through the front door. Perna was right, she thought. The common room was immaculate. The eating table was shiny. The chairs were all pushed into place. The cushions on all of the divans were clean and neat. "We have to keep that boy around!" Sarah remarked with satisfaction.

She walked into the airy courtyard, where a pot of vegetable soup was boiling on the stove. Sarah looked inside and laughed aloud. He may be a good housekeeper, but he needs some cooking lessons, she thought as she started fishing whole vegetables out of the pot. First, Sarah took out foot-long green beans and tenderly cut them into bite-size pieces. Then, she extracted the whole head of cabbage which Elihu had thrown into the pot and chopped it finely. Lastly, she retrieved the four ears of corn, cob and all, and scraped the kernels back into the pot.

Soon the two boys wandered back into the house. Noticing that his mother had set the table, Methuselah yelled, "It sure smells good, Mom. I can't wait to eat Elihu's vegetable soup." After washing up in the courtyard, the two lads sat down to a delicious bowl of piping hot soup. Sarah prayed and then everybody dove into their bowls. Elihu was pleasantly surprised at the bite-size green beans, the cut-up cabbage leaves, and corn without the cob. He meekly looked at Sarah, who just winked and sweetly smiled.

As for Methuselah, he didn't pause or look up until his bowl was empty. "Mmmm, good! That sure was great soup! Mom, Elihu sure can cook, can't he?" Elihu chuckled as Methuselah asked for a second bowl.

## Chapter Three

# Homecoming, Part Two

The next morning Elihu and Methuselah led the sheep out of the sheepcote for a trip up to the hills. Elihu was eager to show Methuselah everything he had learned during the past few weeks. Methuselah was eager to climb once again the hills which held so many childhood memories.

Sarah waved to the boys as they crested the hill at the tamarisk grove. Then, for the first time in weeks, she was alone -- without Methuselah, without Enoch, without Crista. Lord, I am so glad that You will never leave me, nor forsake me.

As Sarah turned to go back inside, her eyes paused at the eating table, remembering how Methuselah had knocked over his glass of milk into Crista's lap so many months ago. She laughed to herself at the memory of Methuselah's clumsy effort to wipe up the mess, succeeding only in knocking over Crista's glass. Sarah laughed again at the thought of the family's efforts of trying to clean up the mess. But then, Sarah stopped laughing and began to cry as she wondered if she would ever hear Enoch's or Crista's laughter again.

As days and weeks rolled by, Methuselah's sorrow over his father's absence was eased by Elihu's presence. In the hills together with the sheep, the two boys really grew to know one another and to respect each other's shepherding skills. Sarah also grew fond of young Elihu, unfailingly polite, always helpful in both house and garden. But Elihu was no substitute for Enoch. Her days were long and her nights even longer. The lonely weeks, however, became a time of spiritual growth for Sarah, her faith strengthened as she meditated upon God's mercy. "Great is Thy faithfulness, O God. It is good that I should both hope and quietly wait for the salvation of the Lord."

One day, while the boys were in the hills with the sheep, Elam, Elihu's farmer father, stopped by Enoch's homestead to check on his son. Sarah was happy for any company, even that of the normally taciturn Elam. However, after his usual formal introduction, Elam launched into an attack upon Sarah's husband. "I heard that you and your son returned home without Enoch. That was a fool thing for Enoch to do, leaving you two to journey home alone."

Sarah, momentarily stunned, paused for a moment before chuckling aloud, thinking of how useless her husband had been for months and months after his devastating spiritual and physical injuries suffered in the City of Gom. "Elam," she smiled, "the only wise thing Enoch has done in the last year is go on his search for God."

Elam spat on the ground next to his boot. "What kind of fool talk is that, Sarah? Enoch don't need a new dose of religion. He always had plenty, as far as I could see."

Sarah continued her maddening smile. "Oh, he was religious, Elam, but that is not the same as having a personal relationship with God."

The farmer just shook his head back and forth, not consoled until Sarah shared with him how well his son had been doing as a shepherd and housekeeper. "That Elihu is a good boy, for sure, Sarah, but he's not too smart," he tried to joke. "Anybody who would rather wander the hills tending stupid sheep than farm God's good green earth has rocks in his head."

Sarah assured Elam that her father Meshach, who had been farming longer than Elam had been alive, would agree. As Elam finally said his good-bye, mounted his horse, and trotted up the path, Sarah suddenly became even more lonely.

As the weeks rolled on, Sarah, Methuselah, and Elihu quickly adjusted to the old routines of life. One typically warm, sunny morning, after a hearty breakfast of biscuits, honey, and honeydew melon, Sarah packed up a bag of food for the boys to take on a two or three-day journey to some far hills where the grass had not been overgrazed. As the last baaaa wafted from the hilltop overlooking Enoch's homestead, as the two boys waved their final good-bye, Sarah overcame her loneliness by cleaning house, weeding the garden, and making still another lambswool pillow for her bed, a new one to welcome her husband when, not if, he returned home.

Sarah almost forgot about eating all day long, until the sun began to drop below the hill-side. She hurried inside to fix dinner before she lost the last of the sun's rays, only to be irritated, then unnerved, by the mournful bellow of the ox. "Who could be visiting the house at this time of the day?" she thought with some alarm as she hesitantly walked toward the front door. Peering outside, up the dogwood-lined path toward the darkening tamarisk grove, Sarah stopped breathing. Near the top of the hill, descending slowly, was the figure of a man, not a normal man, but a man whose body seemed to be glowing with an unearthly aura in the gathering twilight.

The terrified woman involuntarily took a step backward, wishing hope beyond hope that her son and Elihu would somehow appear to protect her. Just as she was about to shut the door, the mysterious creature waved his right arm and cried out to her. To her complete amazement, Sarah heard the sweetest voice on the face of the Earth call out just one word: "Sarah!"

Sarah stopped breathing again as her heart leaped to her throat, this time for joy. Looking again at the strangely glowing man, her feet involuntarily moved forward, faster and faster, until she was racing up the hill, where she fell into the warm, welcome embrace of the only man who could take away her loneliness. The first evening star twinkled in the night as Enoch finally returned home.

## Chapter Four

# Enoch's Story

Later that evening, Enoch shared his adventures during his search for Adam . . . and God. Sarah was appalled at Enoch's description of the abominations which daily occurred in the wicked City of Cain; her heart cringed at the thought that some of those abominations could have happened to her long-lost daughter Crista. A dark cloud settled over her heart until the mood was lifted by Enoch's story of Obstinate, the trouser-eating goat. "I was going to wait until the morning to ask you about that patch on your trousers, dear," Sarah giggled. Enoch just grinned as he continued to tell Sarah about their oldest living ancestors -- Adam and Eve. Although disappointed to hear how old and run-down both Adam and Eve and their homestead had become, she marvelled at the good humor and warmheartedness of those first two who had been made in the image of God.

Sarah then shivered as Enoch told the account of his wilderness journey. "Confronting Satan in that desolate place sounds more horrible than my worst nightmare, dear." She was moved to tears as her husband described the blistering sun and sand and his final, frenzied dash up the tallest hill as he searched for the source of those heavenly voices singing "They That Wait Upon the Lord." "Were you dreaming, dear," the concerned wife asked, "when you heard voices in the wilderness?"

The glow that emanated from Enoch's brow was still startling. "I figured that I was dead, especially when I saw the two cherubim coming after me."

"The two what?" exclaimed Sarah. Her husband did his best to describe the two angels hovering over him, then lifting his nearly lifeless body into the azure sky. "Where did they take you?" his enthralled wife asked.

"That's the best part of the story," her husband replied.

"Well, where?"

"To the Garden."

"The garden! What garden?" his exasperated wife demanded. "Don't play riddles with me, Enoch. Do you mean to tell me that there was a garden in the middle of that wilderness?"

"Of course, Sarah," Enoch replied. "The cherubim flew me to the Garden of Eden."

Sarah's jaw dropped, but no sound came out. Enoch grinned a lopsided grin until his wife caught her breath and timidly asked, "You found the Garden of Eden?"

"Well, really, dear, you could say I sort of stumbled upon it."

Sarah shook her head. "Oh, Enoch, some people are going to have real problems believing all of your adventures -- Adam and Eve, Satan, flying creatures, the Garden of Eden. Why, it's almost too much for me."

Enoch held his wife even closer. "Dear, the best part is yet to come. Let me tell you about the beautiful Garden of Eden." Sarah heard her husband's poor description of the cool, flowing river, the lamb and the lion, the thornless rose, and the Tree of Life itself. "In fact, dear, my new staff is a branch from the Tree of Life."

Sarah gasped. "You tore off a branch from the Tree of Life?"

"No, Sarah," her husband explained. "God did."

# Chapter Five

# God's Blessing

Sarah nearly fainted. Gathering her wits, she looked straight into her husband's eyes and timidly asked, "Y-Y-You met God?"

"Right there in the Garden, dear," her husband absently replied, recalling his first encounter with the Living God. "I was so overwhelmed, I just crumbled," he continued, not noticing that his wife was being likewise overwhelmed by this divine manifestation. "Sarah," he said, "God raised me up to meet Him face to face."

Sarah stuttered, "D-D-Dear, is that glow emanating from you a reflection of the glory of God?"

"I don't have any other explanation for it, dear. I have seen God face to face, and He now lives within my heart."

Sarah shrieked. "Oh, Enoch, you really are a believer now?"

Her husband affirmed, "I know that God is, and that He is a rewarder of them that diligently seek Him." The strain of so many weeks of waiting for her husband to return home finally took its toll as Sarah began to weep uncontrollably until she finally fell asleep in her husband's arms.

Sarah awoke quite late the next morning to the smell of biscuits burning. She dashed into the courtyard just in time to see her husband taking a tray of charred biscuits out of the oven. Looking up sheepishly, he mumbled, "I guess it's getting too hot in here."

"Enoch," his wife chided, "I appreciate your new religious fervor, but it's too early in the day for burnt sacrifices." Looking down at the blackened remains of Enoch's attempted breakfast, Sarah chuckled, "Even the birds won't eat this!" Glancing at the table, she saw a glass of fresh squeezed orange juice. "At least you didn't burn the juice." Enoch recovered enough pride to give his wife a fresh morning squeeze, then suggested that they take a late morning walk before he did any more damage in the kitchen.

Strolling along the bank of the stream running behind their home, Sarah enjoyed the sights and sounds and smells of Enoch's homestead more than she had in weeks. She listened in wonder as her husband began to share God's blessing upon him in the Garden of Eden. "Sarah, I don't know how to explain this fully to you, but God has called me to be a prophet."

Sarah, watching a rabbit bound away toward the brush on the other side of the stream, gaily asked: "What's a prophet, dear?"

Enoch gulped. "A man called of God to speak of what he has heard and seen of the living and true God."

His wife let those words flow over her as she continued watching the rabbit race away from her. A thought crowded into her relaxed mind. "You mean telling people the things that you told me last night about you and God in the Garden of Eden?"

Her husband gulped again. "Precisely, dear."

"Well," Sarah replied, "that doesn't sound so bad. I can live with that. To whom are you supposed to speak, Enoch?"

"To all of the children of Adam."

Sarah's feet stopped as the rabbit disappeared in the brush. Turning toward her husband, she gulped. "What do you mean, 'all the children of Adam?'" Her eyes widened as Enoch explained that God wants him to "Go and speak" and to "Go and teach," wherever God leads him. Enoch moved closer to her and wrapped his arms around his wife as her body began to tremble and tears began to roll down her cheeks. All of their years of marriage, she had never balked when Enoch went into the hills, sometimes for weeks, with the sheep. Even when Enoch went off in search of Adam, Sarah supported him, encouraged him, desired what was best for him, no matter what the personal cost to herself. But now, Sarah was facing a new challenge, a challenge bigger than she or any woman had ever faced. Choking back her tears, she looked directly into her husband's eyes, blue as the beckoning sky. “Enoch, I’m scared. Hold me tight.”

As her husband held her, Sarah gazed beyond the sky toward the home of Him Who had watched over her for so many weeks while she waited for her husband to finally come home. And now, he was talking of leaving again, going out into the world to tell people about the living and true God, to tell people who didn’t care and wouldn’t listen, people like Arphaxad and all of those evil, wicked people in the City of Cain. Her husband held her tighter as she shuddered violently and wept uncontrollably.

Enoch, too, looked longingly into the late morning sky, realizing fully for the first time what sacrifices his family must make in order for him to fulfill God’s calling. But God’s calling is God’s blessing, and Enoch remembered the second blessing. “Honey,” he said soothingly as he stroked his wife’s beautiful black hair, “God’s second blessing is good news. He told me that we should not fear the Evil One, for greater is He that is with us than he that is in the world.”

Sarah shuddered one final time at the thought of her husband facing Evil incarnate in the wilderness, wondering what battles Enoch would wage in the future. She gathered enough strength to ask her husband when he would be leaving. Her husband tried to brighten her gloom as he explained that God told him to wait until God raised up a traveling companion for him. Her gloom almost vanished, then returned with a vengeance, as the thought came unbidden to her mind: Is God going to take Methuselah away from me, too? She turned on her husband. "Wh-who is your traveling companion, Enoch?"

Enoch was almost knocked over by his wife's glare. "Honestly, dear, I don't have a clue."

His wife's heart beat less rapidly as she sarcastically added, "I don't know how much more of God's blessing I can take, Enoch."

Enoch's mind was racing, trying to find something to say to encourage his wife. Then, he thought of the first part of the next blessing of God. "Dear, God also told me that Methuselah will live a very long, long time."

"Great, just great," his wife snapped. "I am sure that my only son will be a comfort to me in my old age while you are gallivanting across the countryside trying to save the world. What else did God tell you about our son?"

Enoch replied unthinking: "God said that, in due time, He would also call Methuselah to be a prophet." He desperately wished he could have yanked those words back as he helplessly watched his wife faint in his arms.

## Chapter Six

# God's Blessing Continued

Enoch gently laid his wife down on the bank of the stream. He scooped some cool water in his hands and sprinkled it in her face. Sarah revived quickly and sat up. "I'm sorry, dear," she softly said, embarrassed at her weakness.

"Oh, Sarah, don't apologize," Enoch said comfortingly. "One thing that I learned from Eve is that it is a godly thing for a woman to have a mother's heart. I wouldn't want you to be any other way."

"Oh, Enoch," Sarah cried as she clung to him: "Do you think Methuselah will be your traveling companion?"

Enoch was kind. "I don't think so, dear, but I really don't know for sure. We will know in God's time."

Sarah continued to sit on the bank. "This is a pretty spot, Enoch. Maybe we should just rest here as you continue to share God's blessing with me."

As the reunited couple sat on the peaceful shore, Enoch related the rest of the blessings that God Almighty had promised to him. He told his incredulous wife that the Lord said that Methuselah was to have a son named Lamech and that Lamech was to have a son named Noah, who was to be a preacher of righteousness. Sarah marveled at these two wonderful pieces of news.

"Noah," Sarah rolled that name around in her mouth. "Noah. I like that name. I can't wait to see him!"

"Hold on, Sarah, we haven't even married off Methuselah yet."

"I can wait. What's next?"

"The sixth blessing is both a curse and a blessing. God will execute judgment upon the corrupted children of Adam, but in His mercy, He will save Noah and his family."

For a moment, Sarah and Enoch speculated as to what form God's judgment might take. Then, eager to hear the rest of the blessing Sarah interrupted Enoch to ask him to finish his narrative.

"Blessing number seven is that in the fullness of time the Redeemer will come and --"

Sarah interrupted again. "Oh Enoch, you must surely tell the whole world that wonderful news. I guess I will have to let you go now."

Sarah was so excited as she thought of Enoch telling large crowds the good news of the coming Redeemer. While she daydreamed, Enoch finished his sentence: "God said that the Redeemer shall descend from Noah."

Sarah's mouth dropped open as she realized the meaning of Enoch's words. She gasped:

"You mean that the Redeemer shall descend from you -- and me?"

Enoch grabbed Sarah quickly, afraid that she would faint again. She quickly assured him that she was fine and began to praise the Lord for His mercy and goodness in choosing their family as ancestors of the coming Redeemer. Sarah was so intent on pouring her heart out to God that she scarcely heard Enoch say quietly: "Sarah, there is one more blessing."

"Oh, Enoch, God has blessed us enough. What more could He do for us than to send the Redeemer?" Sarah's thoughts were on things above, not on things on the Earth. She gazed skyward, looking for that blessed hope and glorious appearing of the Redeemer.

"Sarah, I hate to interrupt your thoughts, but God's eighth and final blessing is more immediate, concerning our own lives, dear. It is one of the desires of your heart. Sarah, God's final blessing is this -- Before I leave this Earth, I will be reunited with Crista!"

Sarah looked into Enoch's eyes, fervently hoping that his eyes confirmed the truth of what he said. When she saw his sincerity, she laid down on the grass and wept tears of joy until she could weep no more.

## Chapter Seven

# Disappointment, Sacrifice, and Miracle

Life never returned to normal at Enoch's home. Enoch and Sarah decided that they would ask Elam's permission for Elihu to permanently move in to help tend the sheep, especially when Enoch was away on his preaching journeys. Sarah saw Elihu as the older brother that Methuselah never had. They determined to ask Elam as soon as they could.

Meanwhile, Enoch was excited about the lads' return from the hills. Sure enough, two days later, Enoch heard the bleating of sheep. Methuselah's joy in seeing his father was overwhelming. Enoch was amazed at how much his son had grown, both in height and maturity. It was a good homecoming.

In the common room that evening, Enoch shared the account of his journeys with the boys. At first, they were spellbound. However, when Enoch began to share God's blessings, Methuselah gradually withdrew. It was obvious that Methuselah did not approve of God's call upon Enoch. He just wanted his daddy at home.

Enoch and Sarah were so wrapped up in Enoch's storytelling that they did not notice their son's reaction. Enoch thought that his son would be excited that God was going to raise up a traveling companion and that God would also call Methuselah to preach. When Enoch turned to his son and asked: "Well, what do you think, son?" Methuselah screamed: "I can't stand it. I don't want to hear anymore!"

Enoch was dumbfounded. Elihu was rooted to the divan, feeling very awkward in the midst of a family squabble. Methuselah bolted out the door, his mother vainly calling him back.

Enoch sat silently, his spirit crushed. Finally, Elihu hesitantly offered, "Sir, I am very sorry for what happened. You know, being a prophet is sort of like being a shepherd. We both know how stupid sheep are. People are like that, too. Sheep will follow any shepherd that they get used to. It seems to me that most people follow bad shepherds. What we need, sir, are good shepherds called of God to lead the people."

Enoch mulled over what Elihu had said. Then he got up, walked over to Elihu, and placed his hand on his shoulder. "I sure would like to keep you around, Elihu."

A sense of uneasiness hovered over Enoch's homestead that night. Even several of the sheep bleated sporadically in the darkness. Enoch slept fitfully, worrying about his rebellious son.

The next morning Enoch felt the Spirit of God impress him to conduct a sacrifice to celebrate his safe return and the safety of his family during his journey. Enoch hoped that Methuselah's former enthusiasm for sacrifice would overcome his distaste for God's blessing. Enoch was sharply disappointed when Methuselah did not react to the announcement of the upcoming sacrifice. Instead, Methuselah hung his head as he lingered over a biscuit, seemingly oblivious to his responsibilities in preparing for the sacrifice. Finally, Sarah quietly mentioned: "Hadn't you better attend to the sacrifice, son?"

Methuselah sat sullenly for a minute. Ignoring his mother, he rose from his chair, went out to the shed, grabbed the sacrificial utensils, and began storming up the hill. Before he took ten steps, he stopped, turned to face the house, and yelled defiantly: "I won't get the sheep!"

Sarah was shocked by Methuselah's unbecoming and uncharacteristic conduct. She turned to Enoch, who sat with his eyes closed, disappointed, yet sympathetic towards the plight of his son. Enoch wearily moved to one of the divans and sat with his eyes closed, praying that God would move on the heart of his son.

After the table was cleared, Elihu finally moved to the common room where Enoch sat unmoving. Elihu meekly said: "Sir, I would be honored to select the sheep."

Enoch sat silently, thinking about Elihu's offer. Deciding that he did not want to create any dissension between the boys, he replied: "Thanks, Elihu, but I better do it myself." Enoch arose, walked to the sheepcote, and selected the finest lamb, one without spot or blemish.

Enoch led the lamb, his wife, and Elihu up the hill to the tamarisk grove, where Methuselah was sulking. He did not greet his family or join them when they gathered around the altar. Methuselah did not even close his eyes when Enoch began the service in prayer: "Dear Lord, be merciful to me a sinner."

Methuselah could not help but stare at his father. This prayer sounded so penitent, so personal, so unlike the prayers his father used to pray before his journey in search of God.

"I have sinned against You, and You alone, O Lord."

Methuselah cringed at his father's words. What about me, Dad? Don't you think you have wronged me?

"Forgive me my iniquities, O Lord."

Methuselah thought darkly to himself: I'll never forgive you if you go on a preaching journey.

"Father, forgive the sins of my family, too."

Again, Methuselah's bitterness welled up inside of him. My sins? What have I done wrong? It's you who wants to leave me.

Throughout the service Methuselah was filled with the gall of bitterness, not once comprehending the sins of his heart. When it came time to sacrifice the lamb, Methuselah participated, grudgingly, not from the heart. Enoch felt the deadness of his son's spirit throughout the service. In his concluding prayer, Enoch asked: "Dear God, the heart of man is deceitful above all things, and desperately wicked. Open up the heart, Lord, of any of us who resist Your Spirit. Let each one of us recognize our sinfulness and our need to be cleansed by the blood of the Lamb, by the blood of the coming Redeemer."

"Lord, if any one of us does not truly believe in You, and does not look forward to the blessed hope and glorious appearing of our Redeemer, please, Lord, I beseech You, fill that heart with more grace that he might believe."

Methuselah was truly moved by his father's prayer, but he resisted the Spirit's prompting. He wasn't ready to believe that God would ever send his father away from him.

Elihu was convicted. He knew that there was something missing in his life. Enoch's prayer cut deeply, like a sword cutting into the marrow of his soul. He began to weep softly, recognizing that he had never fully believed in his total sinfulness and total inability to redeem himself. But now, everything was becoming clear. Elihu opened his heart to God. Peace like a river flooded his soul. Tears of joy flooded down his cheeks.

He was not ashamed to cry because he was no longer ashamed of God.

All eyes turned toward the lad. Enoch and Sarah immediately recognized the miraculous work of grace in Elihu's heart, for his face reflected the glory of God. As for Methuselah, he was doubly troubled, disgusted that his friend would cry like a girl and yet fearful that perhaps God would also take his friend away on his father's infernal preaching journeys.

For the rest of the day, Sarah and Enoch rejoiced with the animated Elihu, who bubbled over with question after question about his new-found God, about Heaven, and how to prepare himself on Earth to walk forever with God in Heaven. Methuselah had a terrible day, but his father rejoiced that God had so soon confirmed that, indeed, God had called him to be a prophet, and the power of God rested upon Enoch.

## Chapter Eight

# Elam's Visit

The next morning a rider crested the hill while Elihu and Methuselah were feeding the sheep. "Company coming!" Methuselah yelled out. Sarah and Enoch, who were working in the garden, rose and returned to the front of the house, where they awaited their visitor.

"Elam, old friend!" Enoch gladly exclaimed, "it's so good to see you."

"May my horse graze under your tree?" Elam asked with his usual stiffness.

"Of course, my friend. Then join us inside." Sarah and Enoch quickly went inside to prepare for their visitor. Meanwhile Elihu and Methuselah came running up. Elihu was delighted to see his father; he could not wait to share with his father that he was now a believer.

But Elam was not at all impressed with Elihu's strange announcement that he had finally opened his heart completely up to God. "You've always been a believer, boy, since you were born, same as your sister Adah," Elam snapped. "Who's filling your head with this foolishness?" Methuselah silently agreed with Elam, grateful that somebody sensible was visiting.

As the three entered the front door, Sarah was just entering the common room from the other direction with a tray, a pitcher of orange juice, and some cups. She served the fresh, delicious drink to all of the men, who quickly downed the juice before anybody could talk. Then, Elam spoke up. "I'm glad you made it home, Enoch," Elam said seriously. "I was worried about you."

"God was with me," Enoch replied truthfully. "How did you know I was home?"

"Everybody knows!" Elam blurted out. "You caused quite a stir walking through the City of Gom like some sort of human glowworm. I thought I would come over and see what all the fuss was about," Elam continued. "What caused it, Enoch?"

"God!" replied Enoch simply and sincerely.

"That doesn't tell me anything!" Elam was acutely irritated. "God causes everything, but I have never seen anybody glow!"

"I walked with God, Elam."

"What!?!" Elam exploded. "Walked with God? That sounds a little farfetched, my friend."

"But I did, Elam. I walked with God in the Garden of Eden."

The room fell silent. Elam fervently eyed everyone to see how they were reacting to Enoch's gibberish. He then realized that Sarah, and even worse, his own son seemed to believe Enoch's incredible story.

Finally, Elam asked whether Arphaxad's club did some permanent damage to Enoch's mind.

Instead of being offended, Enoch just laughed. Then Sarah interrupted: "Really, Elam, Enoch is just fine. And he really did walk with God in the Garden of Eden."

"Were you there with him, Sarah?"

"Why, no, but . . ."

"Then how do you know he was really there?" Elam asked triumphantly.

"Elam, I'm shocked," Sarah retorted. "Are you suggesting that Enoch is lying?"

"No, of course not," Elam curtly replied. "I'm merely wondering if Enoch's brain is working quite right. That was a terrible blow to the head."

Sarah became so angry that she was speechless. Enoch began to explain that his only desire was to share his experiences. His listeners could then evaluate their truth.

Elihu had been quiet, but could not restrain himself any longer. "Dad, I've spent the last few days with Enoch. He's a changed man, Dad, and I'm changed, too. I believe what he says about God."

Elam shot back at his son: "I'm worried about you, too, son, believing the ravings of a madman."

Sarah exploded violently. Shrieking at the top of her lungs, she jumped up, ran to the door, swung it open, and yelled at Elam again: "Get out of MY house!"

Elam arose, grabbed Elihu's arm, and yelled: "This house is filled with crazies. Let's go!"

Elihu, for perhaps the first time in his life, rebelled against his father and pulled his arm away.

Elam backhanded his son and ordered him out of the house.

Elihu looked with pleading eyes at Enoch. Enoch peacefully told Elihu that he must obey his father. Elam grabbed Elihu and dragged him bodily out of the house, threw him on the horse, and galloped up the hill at a furious pace.

Enoch sat on the divan and prayed. "Lord," Enoch said, looking Heavenward, "this prophet business sure has its ups and downs."

## Chapter Nine

# Life Continues

Methuselah distanced himself from his father even more. Not only did he fear his father's imminent departure, but he also worried that he would never see his best friend again. It was a very difficult time for the thirteen-year-old lad.

Sarah and Enoch grew closer. Enoch's spiritual warmth and reality became more evident to her every day. Gone was the cold, impersonal, stiff worship of some distant, aloof deity. Now, Enoch seemed to be living each day with God, endeavoring to become more like Him. He even started singing a little tune every day:

All I want to be
    is to be like my Lord.
And all I want to do
    is just to walk with Him.

Soon, Sarah found herself humming and singing along. Enoch called it God's song.

Enoch continued to wonder whom his traveling companion would be. After Elihu became a believer, Enoch had briefly entertained the hope that perhaps faithful Elihu would be the one.

However, Elam's outburst and sudden departure seemed to void that possibility. It also seemed to crush Enoch's dream of Elihu living with them to help tend the sheep. Enoch did not know it then, but God was just teaching him important lessons on waiting on the Lord.

Enoch was also curious about God's plan for Methuselah, who did not yet appear to be a budding prophet. Perhaps God wasn't going to raise up Methuselah as his traveling companion. Enoch was perplexed but patient.

There were quite a few chores to do in the house and in the garden. There were crops to be planted and harvested, furniture to be repaired, and much, much more. From time to time, other visitors stopped by Enoch's homestead. Enoch was always eager to share with them what he had heard and seen of God. As expected, reactions varied. Some people ranted and raved as Elam had done, while others were more polite. Enoch was a little disappointed that no one came to the Lord as Elihu had done; but Enoch figured that God had a purpose in that, too. So Enoch just worked and walked and waited on the Lord, always ready to go, but responsible enough to take care of the daily, mundane chores around the house. "Just one day at a time," he often heard Sarah say.

Enoch and Methuselah took several trips into the hills with the sheep. Methuselah relaxed more out there, and slowly the tension between him and his father lessened. While Methuselah never worshipped his father as he had done before, at least he learned to respect him for his goodness and especially for his skill as a shepherd.

Enoch, too, noticed that Methuselah was becoming more skillful, responsible, and more mature. Enoch made a point of often praising his son at the eating table. In spite of lingering doubts and fears, a tentative but agreeable peacefulness descended upon Enoch's homestead.

The harvest season soon ended, and it was shearing time. Enoch and son took to the task with evident glee. On the last day of shearing, both father and son were rushing to finish. Methuselah was getting tired of clipping, so he and Enoch changed positions. As Methuselah reached for one of the few remaining woolly sheep, he accidentally stepped on its front hoof. The sheep bleated loudly, causing Methuselah to stumble into the gate, causing it to swing open. The sheep darted through the gate, past Methuselah.

"Shut the gate!" Enoch cried out. Before any more sheep could escape, Methuselah managed to slam the gate shut.

"After him!" Enoch cried out again. The sheep escapee dashed toward the house. Sarah, alerted by the cries, came rushing out of the house, startling the poor, little sheep, who turned and ran through Sarah's beloved herb garden, destroying everything in its path.

"Stop that monster!" Sarah shrieked, and she, too, joined in the chase. The sheep ran to the stream and waded through it, then turned left. Methuselah, followed by his father and mother, splashed through the stream. Then the sheep crossed the stream again and headed straight for the vegetable garden. "Oh, no!" Sarah shrieked again.

The sheep came to the garden hedge. It was so frightened that it crashed right through the hedge, with the three angry humans in hot pursuit. Enoch had enough presence of mind to order Sarah to stay at the new hedge opening and to order Methuselah to cover the garden entrance at the other end. Enoch continued chasing that crazed sheep all over the garden, trying to maneuver it toward the waiting Methuselah. Suddenly, the poor sheep, thoroughly bewildered, charged straight for Methuselah.

It's eyes were glazed as it bore down upon the boy. With a mighty lunge, the sheep butted Methuselah in the stomach, knocking all of the air out of his lungs and throwing the lad ten feet backward. The sheep, stunned by the impact, fell right on top of the breathless Methuselah. Enoch rushed up and lifted the unconscious sheep from his son's body. Sarah dashed to the fallen hero to make sure that he was still alive. "Methuselah! Methuselah! Are you all right?"

The boy lay there for a moment, still unable to breathe. Then he opened his eyes, took a long, deep breath, looked up at his mother and pleaded: "Did we get him?"

Sarah laughed with relief. "Yes, son, you got him." Sarah helped her son get up, then they both assisted Enoch, who was examining the poor sheep. "Is he going to be all right, Dad?"

"Sure, son," Enoch chuckled. "He's just had a little too much excitement for one day."

"So have we," added Methuselah.

"Yes, we have, son. You did a good job of tackling that sheep."

"It's more like he tackled me," chuckled Methuselah.

As the three humans led one slightly dazed sheep back to the sheepcote, Enoch shared a thought with his family. "I wonder if God sees us the same way that we saw this wayward sheep today."

"What do you mean, Dad?"

"All we like sheep have gone astray."

## Chapter Ten

# The Night Before

Soon all of the sheared wool was ready to take to market. The night before the trip to town, tension was evident in Enoch's home. Neither father nor mother, much less Methuselah, seemed willing to express their fears. Dinner was a strangely quiet time as all three were afraid to talk in fear that the dreaded topic might come up.

Finally, Enoch broke the silence. "It will be strange going back to the City of Gom." Neither Sarah nor Methuselah responded, afraid to express the inevitable. Enoch felt like he must force the issue, so he kept talking. "It will be good to see Ludim again. I hope he is more responsive to my stories about God than Elam was."

Again, Methuselah and his mother were silent. "Oh, come on, you two," Enoch said with desperation, "talk to me. It's not like tomorrow is the end of the world."

"I hope not," Sarah said softly, temporarily breaking her reign of silence. Enoch then wished he had not said his last sentence. With an air of resignation, he went back to his food.

The rest of the evening was no better for Enoch. Both his wife and son were sullen and withdrawn. Just before bedtime, Methuselah finally spoke to his father. "Dad, you don't want me going to town with you tomorrow, do you?"

Enoch gazed upon the sad countenance of his thirteen-year-old boy. Methuselah looked as eager as a slain sacrificial lamb. "I need your help, son," Enoch replied, "and I sure could use your company. This trip will be as hard on me as it will be on you."

Methuselah did not respond verbally. With fearful eyes, he turned and slowly walked away, his mind numb with the thought of going back to the place of his most agonizing defeat in life. Enoch nearly wept as his son seemed to drift away.

Enoch slept fitfully that night. Shortly before dawn, when the night was at its blackest, Enoch was awakened by a familiar voice. Enoch opened his eyes and saw Sarah was fast asleep at his side and did not awaken.

Then the word of the Lord came unto him, saying: "Fear not, Enoch. Tomorrow shall be your first journey for My glory. Before I formed thee in the belly I knew thee; and before thou camest forth out of the womb I sanctified thee. I ordained thee a prophet unto all the children of Adam."

Then the Lord put forth His hand and touched Enoch's mouth. "Behold, I have put My words in thy mouth."

Enoch was stunned. He stumbled out of bed, and prostrated himself at his Lord's feet.

The Lord took Enoch's arm and raised him up. Face to face, the Lord continued to instruct His reluctant prophet: "I have given you the staff of God from the Tree of Life. Lean on Me! I have this day set thee over the people, to pull down, and to destroy, to build, and to plant. Through you, I will utter my judgments against the people who have forsaken Me, and burned incense unto other gods, and worshipped the works of their own hands."

The Lord's words overpowered Enoch. "O Lord, I am Your servant," Enoch said weakly, "but what of people like Zaava or even Elam? They will surely think that I am mad. They might even try to kill me."

God's lovingkindness and tender mercies were tempered with justice: "Be not dismayed or afraid of their faces, Enoch, lest I confound thee before them."

God's words shook Enoch to his bones: "Enoch, I am with thee to deliver thee. For, behold, I have made thee this day a defensed city, against all of the children of Adam. And they shall fight against thee; but they shall not prevail."

Those words rang in Enoch's ears as the Lord disappeared from sight. For hundreds of years, Enoch often returned his thoughts to the memory of that special night. Not until later did Enoch realize the full meaning of God's words. Wherever Enoch journeyed though, he took with him the promises and the staff of God.

## Chapter Eleven

# Return to the City of Gom

The next morning at breakfast Enoch shared his vision of the Lord with his family. Methuselah was quite skeptical, and attributed it to a bad dream caused by indigestion.

Sarah, on the other hand, believed immediately. A new and higher respect for Enoch and his calling, and a stronger faith in the keeping power of God, swelled in her heart.

Nonetheless, Sarah was tearful as Enoch and Methuselah said their good-byes and rode up the hill. But her heart told her that Enoch would be back.

On the way to town, Methuselah studiously avoided speaking to his father. Enoch did not want to interrupt his son's apparent reverie, but finally spoke up: "I know that you are disappointed in God's call upon me to be a prophet, son."

Methuselah slowly turned his eyes away from the forest, relieved that he could talk out his feelings. "I guess I'm scared more than anything else, Dad," Methuselah confessed. "What will people do when they hear you speak?"

"God has promised," Enoch meekly replied, "that He will be with me to deliver me. Can't you trust Him?"

"Maybe," the young lad replied. "But what about Mom and me? Will God be with us while you are gone?"

Methuselah continued to press his arguments. "And Dad, why can't all of your journeys be short like this one? Why would you have to preach elsewhere? Don't people around here need to hear the Words of God?"

Enoch was thoughtful for a minute. "I am grateful, son, that my first journey for God is so nearby. But God called me to preach to all of the children of Adam. If God keeps me close to home, so be it. But if He sends me to faraway places, I must go."

"Well, I hope God keeps you close to home," Methuselah continued to insist.

Enoch did not reply directly, but started to sing the song that he had sung so much recently.

All I want to be
    is to be like my Lord.
And all I want to do
    is just to walk with Him.

Enoch sang the song through a couple of times, then turned toward his son. "Methuselah, the most important thing a believer can do in this world is to walk with God. If God wants me to walk with Him here, then I can't walk with Him anywhere else. And if God wants me to walk with Him somewhere else, then I can't walk with Him here." The young lad was quiet as he mulled over his father's last words. Then he returned his gaze to the forest.

Later, Enoch and Methuselah drove into the City of Gom. The city held no attraction for Methuselah. It reminded Enoch of the City of Cain as he drove through the market, for merchants were now selling butchered meat of all sorts. Enoch felt a strong, natural tendency to just scream out "God forbid!" Instead, he just commented to his son: "Next, they'll have prostitutes and a slave market."

Enoch watered the ox at the fountain, unnoticed by the bustling crowd. He then drove the wagon to Ludim's house. The beloved blacksmith welcomed Enoch as a long-lost brother. Methuselah was relieved that Ludim forgot to give him a bearhug. Ludim was thrilled beyond measure that Enoch was now a true believer. Both Ludim and Perna sat spellbound as Enoch told them tales of Adam and Eve, the Garden of Eden, and God Himself. When Enoch finally told the part of his testimony of how God had called him to be a prophet, Ludim raised his eyes Heavenward and cried out: "Thank You, Lord, for answering my prayer!"

Then Ludim turned back to Enoch and explained that Perna and he had been praying for months that God would raise up a prophet, a champion to battle the forces of evil overtaking their city.

Enoch was stunned by Ludim's revelation. "Perhaps," Enoch thought out loud, "God called me to be a prophet only in answer to your prayers." While Enoch marveled at the power of prayer, young Methuselah felt only resentment toward Ludim and Perna that they may have had something to do with his father leaving home.

While the men kept talking, Perna brought in some fresh baked biscuits. Enoch was enjoying the food but not the news on the latest transgressions to occur in the city. "You can see the extent of the animal market, Enoch. Almost everybody in the city is eating meat now." Enoch stopped chewing for a moment and just sighed as Ludim continued. "My wayward son Tubal is the main benefactor. Most of the animal merchants work for him." Then Ludim reluctantly added: "Your brother Aram also works for Tubal now."

Enoch rather impolitely spit out his biscuit on his plate. "Oh no, not Aram!" Enoch cried, lowering his head in his hands. Enoch slowly looked up and asked: "Is he here now?"

"No," Ludim replied, "he's off with Tubal on one of his infernal business trips." Enoch just shook his head as Ludim continued. "Zaava is becoming bolder. Introducing meat eating was just the start of her iniquity. Now she is actively promoting the worship of that wicked ebony cow which she keeps in her so-called secret chamber."

Ludim went on to detail yet another abominable practice that the wayward citizens had begun -- a slave market. He explained that the slave market is held on the east platform of the city gate, the same place where the debate debacle was held last year.

Enoch was quiet and prayerful. Methuselah was afraid of what his father might be thinking. Then Enoch spoke: "God wants me to speak out against this new evil today."

Although Methuselah protested, Enoch was fearless. He thundered: "Last year, when I stood up to Arphaxad and spoke out against evil, I failed because I stood up in the power of the flesh. But this time, I shall go in the name of the Lord, armed only with the promises and staff of God."

"Be careful, my brother," cautioned Ludim.

"Ludim, you and Perna are powerful prayer warriors. Please pray for me now."

"We shall, Enoch, especially considering who the chief slave merchant is."

"Who's that?" Enoch asked.

"Arphaxad!"

## Chapter Twelve

# Arphaxad

After a holy time of prayer, Enoch and Methuselah drove the wagon to the marketplace. Most of the places were filled, but Enoch found an empty space not far from the fountain. For about an hour Enoch successfully traded wool for a variety of household and garden items. Methuselah was relieved that nothing had gone wrong yet.

Methuselah's musings were interrupted by the clanging of the gong. All eyes turned to the east platform. There stood a little girl, no older than Crista, and two of the thugs which Methuselah had seen last year. Then, ascending the steps to the platform was the tall, broad figure of Arphaxad. A great fear seized Methuselah.

All activity in the marketplace ceased as Arphaxad began to speak: "Listen up, you sniveling cowards! This is the mighty Arphaxad speaking!" The voice grated upon Methuselah's ears and brought back terrible memories. "I am really disappointed in you idiots," the bully continued. "I came here yesterday with six slaves and I only sold five of them."

Arphaxad reached over, grabbed the little girl by the hair, and jerked her next to him. "Now listen, you spineless weaklings, I know that this little runt isn't the greatest prize, but I'm not taking her back with me. If one of you wealthy citizens does not buy her today, then I will simply slit her throat."

Enoch gasped, appalled at Arphaxad's words. The gathered crowd, which was silent for a moment, started to grow restless under Arphaxad's relentless stare.

Enoch felt great pity for the poor girl on the platform. What would the crowd do? Then, Enoch was amazed when someone in the crowd shouted: "Go ahead and kill her."

Arphaxad smiled viciously. "What an honorable group of people the city dwellers of Gom are," he said sarcastically. "I would be happy to oblige. But first, let me raise the price. If someone does not buy her, not only will I kill her, but my friends and I will go out into the crowd and kill one of you!"

Now the crowd gasped in horror. Just the day before, out of fear, the city dwellers had permitted Arphaxad to begin a slave market. Arphaxad continued to play upon that fear.

Enoch was ready to move forward. Suddenly Ludim appeared at his side. "I will be praying for you, my brother." As Enoch made his way through the crowd, he could hear several frightened merchants making bids for the little girl.

"I'll give you a lamb," one voice cried out.

"Ha!" replied Arphaxad. "I want more!"

Another merchant quivered: "I'll give you two lambs!"

"More!" the thug insisted.

"I'll give you one ounce of gold," a customer replied, as the crowd seemed to overcome its reluctance and entered into the spirit of bidding.

"Do I hear two ounces?" Arphaxad yelled with glee.

The next bid stunned Arphaxad and the crowd. "I'll give you nothing but the wrath of God!"

All eyes turned toward the incredibly bold speaker. When the city dwellers saw who it was, they bolted away from him as if he had leprosy. Standing alone, with the promises and staff of God, facing Arphaxad and his two friends, stood Enoch.

Arphaxad laughed in derision. "Why, if it isn't the Sheep Man! I heard that you were still alive. How unfortunate."

Enoch was bold. "In one sense, the old Enoch is dead, Arphaxad. I am a new man, more alive than ever before, by the grace of God."

Arphaxad continued to mock. "So the Sheep Man is a new man, by-the-grace-of-God," the thug slowly spit out the last words. "Well, well, well. Listen up, Sheep Man! By the grace of Arphaxad, the new Enoch is going to die today." Then Arphaxad motioned to his two friends: "Take him, boys!" They started to move toward the steps.

Just then, Enoch could hear the still, small voice of God: "Lean on Me, Enoch, lean on Me!"

Before the two men on the platform could take another step, Enoch waved the staff of God over his head. Immediately a bolt of light shot through the sky and a loud rumble, like stampeding cattle, filled the air. Arphaxad's gang froze in their tracks, unable to move.

After a few moments, Arphaxad's mouth began to move. He cleared his voice twice before he could form words. As he finally spoke, his mocking tone was replaced by sheer terror. "Listen up, Sheep Man. I don't know how you did that, but if you don't leave now, I will slit this little girl's throat." He raised his knife.

The little girl was absolutely petrified. The crowd responded to Arphaxad's words and focused their eyes upon Enoch. Then Enoch replied sternly: "The power you saw was not my power, but God's. That same God shall judge you this day, Arphaxad!"

Arphaxad had never heard such threats in his life. As Enoch moved a step forward, the terrified thug screamed out: "Stop or I'll kill her!"

Enoch stopped, closed his eyes, and prayed aloud: "O God, strike this man down." Then Enoch raised his staff, waved it over his head, and pointed it right at Arphaxad. Again, with a loud rumble, a bolt of light streaked through the air.

Arphaxad tried to dodge, but it caught him in the neck. The stricken bully spun around, dropped his knife, and the girl, then toppled off the platform to the street below.

Enoch walked through the crowd which was rooted in place, to the body of Arphaxad, knelt to discover that he was still breathing, then climbed the platform steps. He took the hand of the little girl, checked to see that she was all right, then stated: "God has spoken. He has judged Arphaxad for the evil which he brought upon our city. And God will judge you for the evil which you bring and which you permit." Just then, as Enoch scanned the marketplace, he spied the approaching figures of Zaava, and her lackey Lalomar. Zaava's face was contorted, as Enoch spoke even more boldly.

"Your iniquity is before you. First, you have permitted, then embraced meat eating. That sin, like a cancer, has spread. Then today, you permitted a slave market in your city. If you do not turn from your wicked ways now, next you will embrace slavery."

The eyes of some of the city dwellers looked down in shame as Enoch spoke. "Another evil has befallen the City of Gom. Some people have burned incense to other gods and worshipped the works of their own hands. God will deal severely with this iniquity."

Enoch looked straight into Zaava's eyes, and boldly concluded: "I have walked with God. He wants you to turn from your wicked ways and walk with Him, too."

Just then, Zaava managed to yell: "Don't listen to this madman!" Her words rang throughout the marketplace. Emboldened by her words, several others in the crowd, men who worshipped another god in Zaava's chamber, took up the chant.

A fear gripped even Enoch. But then he remembered God's words: "They shall fight against thee, but they shall not prevail against thee; for I am with thee to deliver thee." Comforted and emboldened, Enoch raised his arm and waved his staff. For the third time that afternoon, a loud rumble and a bolt of light filled the sky. The mouths of the hecklers were stopped immediately. The crowd was motionless as Enoch led the little girl down the steps of the platform. The crowd parted as Enoch and the girl walked toward Ludim and Methuselah. Enoch placed the girl's hand in Methuselah's hand and directed him to wait at the wagon.

Then Enoch asked Ludim to follow him. The crowd watched as they picked up the unconscious body of Arphaxad and carried him to Enoch's wagon. As Enoch drove the wagon back towards Ludim's house with the thug as cargo, the crowd began to disperse. The two remaining men on the platform were finally able to move, quickly disappearing through the city gate.

## Chapter Thirteen

# Decisions

"That was quite a show you put on back there," observed Ludim as Enoch drove the wagon back to the blacksmith shop.

"No, my friend," Enoch replied, "that was God's show, not mine."

The two friends quickly fell to discussing the miracles God did through Enoch. Ludim wanted to know how Enoch made the loud noise and bright light erupt from his staff. After Enoch confessed his complete ignorance with regard to that issue, they shared a moment of praise to God, Who is faithful in all things and Who keeps His promises.

Then Enoch turned to the back of the wagon, looked at the still body of Arphaxad, and asked Methuselah about the little girl they rescued.

Methuselah was still holding the little girl's hand as she sat very close to him. He was both embarrassed and sympathetic toward the young girl. He was also grateful that his father was able to save her from the evil clutches of the slave trader. Methuselah looked up at his dad and replied: "I think she is going to be all right."

Just then, the girl looked up at Enoch's son and said: "Methuselah! That's a nice name."

Methuselah blushed, speechless. Enoch turned toward the girl and asked: "What's your name, little girl?"

Then the little girl lowered her head and replied softly: "Martha."

"Martha! That's a nice name. How old are you, Martha?" Enoch asked.

"Twelve."

Methuselah winced slightly. Crista was twelve years old when he saw her last, in this same marketplace. Now, it seemed as if God had brought another twelve-year-old girl into his life.

Enoch, too, was touched. He looked wistfully at the young girl and reassured her that everything would be all right. Both Enoch and his son were lost in their thoughts as the ox pulled the wagon on towards Ludim's house.

Perna rushed out to meet them. Ludim assigned Perna to get Martha situated as Ludim and Enoch carried Arphaxad to Tubal's old room. Perna's curiosity at the identity of the wounded stranger immediately turned to horror when her husband matter-of-factly informed her that is was Arphaxad. Then her inbred hospitality took over, and she hurried to bring the necessary medical supplies.

Ludim examined Arphaxad's neck wound. "It's bad, Enoch. It's like he was sliced with an incredibly sharp knife. And some dirt must have gotten into it when he fell on the road." When Perna arrived with clean cloths, her husband, with hundreds of years of experience of cleaning and patching up wounded animals, quickly cleaned out the wound as best he could with hot water. Arphaxad's body did not even react to the almost boiling water. Then the blacksmith put some horse liniment inside the wound and quickly stitched it up with cat whiskers.

The neck operation completed, Ludim rolled the limp body of Arphaxad over on the side and stripped off his shirt. A deep purple bruise spread across Arphaxad's back. "Just as I thought, Enoch. Arphaxad landed directly on his back after falling a good fifteen to twenty feet. He must be seriously hurt. That is why his body did not react at all to the hot water, the liniment, or the needle and stitches." Ludim then rolled the body back over on its back.

"What can we do for him, Ludim?" Enoch asked.

"There's not much we can do. We need to keep an eye on that neck wound."

"How long will it take before he gets better?" Perna asked hesitantly.

"Don't know if he will get better. He may die before nightfall, or be paralyzed, or live to be a thousand years old," Ludim responded.

"What will we do with him if he lives?" Enoch quizzed.

Ludim looked down at the seemingly lifeless body. "I almost wish he wouldn't live, but his life is in God's hands, not ours. My chief concern is with his safety, not his health."

"What do you mean, dear?" Perna asked with a puzzled look.

"The way I look at it, some of the brave city dwellers might get their courage up now that Arphaxad is badly wounded. They might want to lynch him."

Perna looked at Enoch. "Well, if you ask me, any man who kidnaps little girls deserves to be hanged. Don't you think so, Enoch?"

Enoch seemed lost in thought. Then he responded slowly: "I may agree with you that Arphaxad deserves to be hanged, but not by some city-dweller lynch mob."

"I agree, Enoch," Ludim piped in. "So what do we do with our patient?"

Enoch puzzled over that question for a minute while Ludim and Perna looked on. Suddenly, Enoch was possessed with a strange idea. "I've got it. If Arphaxad lives through the night, I'll take him with me!"

"Where are you going to take him?" Ludim questioned with some suspicion in his voice.

"Home!"

Perna fainted. Ludim grabbed her before she hit the floor. Enoch helped Ludim ease Perna into the chair in Tubal's bedroom. Ludim ran to get some cool water from the kitchen while Enoch fanned Perna's face. She quickly recovered and looked up at the concerned men. With a quiver in her voice, she reassured the men that she was fine -- except for her hearing.

She spoke again with real affection in her voice. "Enoch, I have known you since you were born. God truly has blessed you with a wonderful wife. Your lovely Sarah has so many godly virtues. But I am afraid that she will never stand for having the kidnapper of her daughter as a patient in her house."

Enoch was ready with an answer which could not have come from within himself. "Perna, don't you see? Arphaxad is the only person who can help me to find Crista."

Enoch's reasoning dumbfounded Ludim. "You are crazy, Enoch. Why should a reprobate character like Arphaxad want to help you?"

"Maybe he will be grateful if we nurse him back to health."

Ludim could only laugh. "You ask for miracles, my friend."

"Yes, I do, my fellow believer. And we know Someone Who can perform them."

Ludim laughed again. "Amen, prophet Enoch, Amen! God can do the impossible." Ludim then escorted his wife and friend out of the bedroom to check on little Martha.

Martha was fast asleep on the divan while Methuselah was busy stuffing cookies into his mouth. "Ummm," Methuselah managed to mumble, "I found a little something to munch on while you were taking care of that miserable thug.

Martha fell asleep and I-well-I needed something to do."

Perna smiled sweetly. "I made those just for you, Methuselah."

Ludim, Enoch, and Perna began to discuss what should be done with Martha. Ludim suggested that Enoch take her home to Sarah, but Enoch demurred. Just then Perna mentioned that they could raise Martha since none of their own grandchildren were close by. They decided to pray about the whole situation and talk to Martha in the morning.

## Chapter Fourteen

# On The Way Home

"I hope Arphaxad dies tonight!" Methuselah adamantly stated.

Enoch's heart broke as he tried to counsel his impetuous son. He reminded Methuselah that Arphaxad could provide the only way to find Crista. Methuselah was bent on revenge, however, and didn't heed his father's advice, stating sullenly, "I don't believe in miracles, Dad."

Enoch felt that he was failing as a spiritual leader of his household. The great victory at the city gate was now being followed by a bitter family defeat. "Son," Enoch said with resignation, "I truly want what is best for you, your mother, and your sister. Perhaps you will not always understand why I am doing something. Sometimes, as I seek to walk closely with the Lord, I do not always understand what the Lord is doing." With his mind made up, Enoch concluded: "I am going to pray for God's perfect will in this matter. If Arphaxad dies tonight, God's will be done. If Arphaxad is still breathing early in the morning, before the rising of the sun, then we will take him home with us."

"Dad, I'm going to pray that God takes Arphaxad's life tonight."

"Pray as you must, son." With that benediction, Enoch said that he would see his son in the morning.

Enoch spent hours in prayer that night. With only a couple of hours sleep, Enoch awakened Ludim and Methuselah. When the three of them went into Tubal's room to check on Arphaxad, Methuselah was severely disappointed that he was still breathing. Ludim suggested that they move the bed with Arphaxad in it, so as not to injure him further. With great difficulty, and more than a little reluctance on Methuselah's part, Arphaxad and his bed were carried out to Enoch's waiting wagon. Lifting the heavy cargo into the wagon nearly broke Methuselah's back; he was grateful that Ludim was as big and strong as he was.

"We better cover the bed completely with canvas and bags of wool, just in case some of my neighbors notice you riding out of town. Some people might not take a liking to your pirating Arphaxad out of town before they can hang him."

"Good idea, my friend," said Enoch. "I am sure that Arphaxad will not complain." As Enoch and Methuselah prepared the wagon, Ludim ran back into the house and returned quickly with a basket of biscuits for the journey home.

"Ludim, you have been a great friend. As I head home with my strange cargo, please ask God's blessing." The three bowed their heads with

Ludim beseeching God's mercy and protection, as well as Sarah's understanding and patience.

The wagon left Ludim's yard and headed slowly toward the city gate. No one was about in the marketplace before dawn. Soon, Enoch, Methuselah, and their cargo were on the road home. Methuselah made no attempt at conversation until long after the sun came up. Then he broke the silence with an inquiry as to Martha's fate. After hearing that Ludim and Perna may take her to raise as their own, a grin crept across the lad's face. "You know, Dad, she is kind of nice," he shyly said. Enoch turned toward his son, tousled his hair, and marveled at the resiliency of youth.

Methuselah spoke again: "Dad, I'm sorry about last night. I was a little hard on you. Can you forgive me?"

As Enoch silently thanked the Lord for answering one of his prayers, he grinned at his quickly maturing son, and nodded happily.

Methuselah sat quietly a minute as the ox continued to plod toward home. Then he brightly announced: "I was really proud of you yesterday, Dad. That was really exciting how you defeated Arphaxad."

Enoch swallowed hard, and then managed to say: "I am proud to have you as my son." When Methuselah looked in his father's eyes and realized that his father really meant those words, the newly reconciled father and son shared a hug.

The topic of conversation turned to Sarah's reaction to her strange patient. Methuselah requested that he have a chance to tell Sarah what happened at the city gate.

Enoch thought that was a great idea. For the rest of the ride home, Enoch and his son sang songs, talked about the beautiful forest, and enjoyed each other's company.

## Chapter Fifteen

# Arphaxad's Terror

Methuselah's plan was working perfectly as he shared the exciting adventure of the previous day with his mother in the common room while all three of them were sipping fresh orange juice. Sarah cried as Methuselah told of how Enoch had rescued the little girl from Arphaxad's evil clutches. "I hope that Arphaxad burns in Hell forever," Sarah said with disgust. At that point, Methuselah's plan started falling apart. "Did you bury that thug yesterday, Enoch?"

Enoch looked for help from his son as he stammered, "Uh-well-uh, sort of, but actually, Arphaxad did not die yesterday."

Sarah gasped with horror as she turned toward Enoch: "You didn't bury him alive, did you?"

Enoch looked lost. "Well, no, not exactly."

Sarah was becoming perplexed. "Then, where is the body of Arphaxad?"

Methuselah tried to answer honestly: "In the back of our wagon, buried underneath piles of wool."

Sarah nearly swooned. She caught her breath, then weakly said: "Now, let me get this straight. You brought the corpse of Arphaxad all the way from the City of Gom to our homestead? What are you going to do? Bury him or stuff him?"

Enoch suddenly had visions of his showing off a stuffed Arphaxad as a trophy. Enoch started giggling, then Methuselah. In a flash, both father and son became hysterical in front of an increasingly distraught Sarah. Sarah couldn't stand it any longer, so she started to go out the front door to check on Arphaxad's body for herself. Enoch quickly composed himself and stopped his wife just before she got to the wagon.

"Sarah, I need to explain something. Arphaxad was horribly wounded, perhaps fatally, but he was still alive when we set out from Ludim's this morning. We brought him here to nurse him back to health."

Sarah's reaction was predictably explosive. "I will not . . . I will not . . ."

Sheer fury was not abated by Enoch's revelation that God had led him to do this. It was only when Enoch pointed out that perhaps Arphaxad could lead them to Crista that Sarah's face softened momentarily. Enoch pointed out to her: "God wants us to love our enemies, to bless them that curse us, to do good to them that hate us, and pray for them which despitefully use us and persecute us."

Sarah was still skeptical. However, after a few more protests, she began to weep softly as she leaned against her husband's chest. "Oh, Enoch, God has never tested my faith in such a way before." Between sobs, she prayed that God would give her more faith and more strength.

One-half hour later, after much backbreaking strain, Arphaxad, still lying unconscious on Ludim's bed, was resting in one corner of the common room. Sarah truly felt that her home had been violated.

The next few days seemed like a dream, or more like a nightmare, to Sarah. Comatose Arphaxad needed a great deal of special attention. His clothes were wet and foul-smelling from his own filth. Enoch and Methuselah helped to strip his clothes off and helped bathe him. Sarah had to wash his clothes immediately since Enoch's clothes were not nearly big enough for Arphaxad's body.

Then Methuselah said Arphaxad's body must be dehydrating. Try as they could, they could not pour any water down the man's unfeeling throat. Enoch became concerned that Arphaxad might die from thirst.

One night, just before dawn, a groggy Arphaxad finally regained consciousness. His first coherent thought was that he must have a drink. He opened his eyes and could see only darkness. Although he sensed that he was inside a building, he had no idea where. As he shook more cobwebs from his mind, he determined that he must get up and find a drink of water. He could tell that he was lying in bed, so he tried to swing his legs over the side. As he tried to move his legs, a sharp, severe pain shot through his back. He yelled, or tried to, but no sound came from his throat. He just lay there in agony, helpless, dying of thirst.

Soon, a little sunlight peeped in through the windows. As Arphaxad's eyes adjusted, he could tell that he was in the common room of a strange house. Although the room was pleasant enough, Arphaxad was instantly suspicious.

"Whose house am I in?"

As his mind grappled with all of his pain and problems, Arphaxad heard sounds from elsewhere in the house. "Someone else lives here," he thought. He wanted to hide, but he was helpless to move or cry out. He knew he needed help, but Arphaxad never trusted anyone.

He then heard a door open and someone entered the room. "Please give me a drink of water," the helpless man vainly cried out in his mind. The unheeding person did not even look at the motionless body on the bed as he walked with his back to Arphaxad toward the front door. As he swung the door open, a flood of light blinded the bedridden man, who blinked and shut his eyes immediately.

Arphaxad could hear footsteps outside as the person walked around to the right side of the house. He could hear a shout: "Now that is a big orange!" Arphaxad craftily concluded that he was in the countryside somewhere, but where? All he knew was that he wanted a slice of that orange.

He could hear footsteps approach the open front door. "I must get his attention. He must give me something to drink!"

Just then the young man appeared again at the doorway. Arphaxad could not initially make out the face in the shadows of the doorway. As the young man entered the room, Arphaxad followed him intently with his eyes. "Please, please look this way!"

Just as Arphaxad's eyesight adjusted to the room, the young man glanced over at the prone body on the bed. As the young man's eyes glanced at the face, his eyes met the pleading stare of a conscious Arphaxad. When Arphaxad saw the young man's eyes and face at the same time, terror filled the room. "That's Enoch's son!"

## Chapter Sixteen

# The Insulting Patient

Both Methuselah and Arphaxad shrieked as loudly as they could. Only Methuselah's scream, however, could be heard. Methuselah ran straight through the kitchen door, nearly knocking Sarah over. As Arphaxad lay motionless, frantic thoughts of escape raced through his head.

"Mom, Arphaxad's eyes are open! I think he is alive!"

The villain cringed inside. Without thinking clearly, still terrified from the awful discovery that he lay helpless in his adversary's home, Arphaxad thought: "They have found me. They know that I am alive. They are going to come and kill me now."

Enoch came dashing out of the bedroom to meet his family. As they were excitedly relaying the news of Arphaxad's recovery, Arphaxad's mind was reeling.

His eyes were brimming with terror as Enoch, Sarah, and Methuselah carefully entered the common room. As Enoch approached the bed and looked full into the fear-crazed eyes of his daughter's kidnapper, he quietly said, "Fear not, Arphaxad." Then Enoch knelt down beside the bed and started to pray. "Dear God, please restore the health of this injured man. Let him know the power of God to heal the body and the soul. Until the Redeemer comes, Amen!" Just as Enoch raised his head, Arphaxad spit in his face.

"Aha, you see, I am not completely helpless!" the thug triumphantly thought. Methuselah was enraged that the miserable oaf would strike out at his father. The boy raised his arm to batter the helpless patient. "You little pip-squeak!" Arphaxad thought as he braced against the imminent blow. "If I were healthy, I would swat you down like a pesky fly." Suddenly, Enoch intervened. "Peace, my son," the father admonished. "We must give God time to work on our patient." Just then, Arphaxad gathered all of his resources one more time and spit into Methuselah's face.

Enoch then moved his family out of range. "The man must be dying of thirst. Sarah, please get him some water." When Sarah returned, Enoch took the cup and said: "Here, Arphaxad, take just a little sip. It will ease your thirst."

"You can't fool me," the crazed Arphaxad thought. "I know there is poison in that cup." As Enoch lowered the cup toward his mouth, Arphaxad waited, then with a desperate, painful jerk, thrust his head forward, knocking the cup backward into Enoch's face. "I beat you again, Sheep Man," the thug silently exulted.

Sarah couldn't take it any longer. "I have had enough of this man's insults." As she stormed out of the room, followed by Methuselah, Arphaxad's face slowly twisted into a triumphant grin.

"You lying, treacherous hypocrite!" Arphaxad smirked. "You just tried to poison me!" Arphaxad did not know what love was. He only knew hate. He just could not begin to believe that the Sheep Man was sincere.

Suddenly, Enoch had an idea. "Methuselah!" When his son came running, he told him to go out into the orchard and pick a ripe, juicy orange. When Methuselah returned with a large, ripe five-pound orange, Enoch told him to go get a sharp knife.

Arphaxad panicked. He was certain he would be fileted alive, and he would be helpless to prevent it.

When Methuselah returned with a long, very sharp knife, Arphaxad lost all hope. He thought, "I'm dying of thirst. I can see a juicy orange in front of me. Now they are going to kill me." If he knew how to cry, he would have.

Just then, Enoch raised the knife and . . . and . . . started to slice the orange. Arphaxad couldn't believe his eyes. His parched tongue silently cried out: "Give me some of that orange juice. I am going crazy with thirst!"

"Here, son, squeeze some of this orange juice on Arphaxad's lips."

"Dad, I wouldn't get too close to him."

"I knew it!" the crazed Arphaxad cried. "They are just torturing me." Just then Enoch reached over with an orange slice and squeezed a few drops on Arphaxad's parched lips. "Ahhh!" the thug murmured to himself as his tongue licked the life-giving juice. Then Enoch squeezed some more, then more. As Arphaxad lapped up the wonderful orange juice, the thought came to him: "Perhaps, they just want to fatten me up for the slaughter."

Arphaxad slowly began to improve. He started to eat and drink ravenously, seemingly making up for lost meals. He was insulted beyond description that Enoch and his family had to change his bed clothes several times a day. "Just wait until I get out of here. I will kill you for these insults!"

Day after day Arphaxad tried to talk so he could verbally insult his hosts, but his neck wound prevented him from sharing his hatred and disgust. He sneered to himself when they described him as a patient, not a prisoner. For days, Arphaxad filled his mind with clever plots to escape and with fiendish plans to torture and murder this sickeningly sweet and hypocritical family.

## Chapter Seventeen

# Elam's Visitation

As was the family custom, Enoch had devotions with his family every evening in the common room. They would sing and pray and talk about one of the Tales of Father Adam, which Enoch called the Words of God, or Enoch's experiences in the Garden of Eden, or the character and attributes of God. Methuselah, who was not yet a believer, never felt completely comfortable during family devotions. His discomfort, however, was minor compared to Arphaxad's. He was completely outraged, but utterly helpless to prevent family devotions. The only enjoyment Arphaxad received from such devotions was watching young Methuselah squirm at some of the things his father said. "The kid may not be much, but he has more sense than his father."

One day, on a bright and beautiful morning several weeks after Enoch brought Arphaxad home, Elam and Elihu arrived at Enoch's home. "Company coming!" cried out Methuselah. He rejoiced to see Elihu. But Arphaxad's only thought was: "This must be the executioner."

"Let me do the talking, son," Elam sternly said to Elihu as they dismounted. Elihu winked at Methuselah, who came running up from the sheepcote. As Sarah opened the front door to greet her guests, Elam asked stiffly: "May my horse graze under your tree?" Sarah waved her guests on into the common room, where both Elam and Elihu instantly noted the patient lying on a bed in the corner.

Just then Enoch came into the common room from the courtyard, where he had been fixing Sarah's stove. Enoch immediately noticed that his neighbor's face was grim, while Elihu's face was beaming with the joy of his salvation and his glee at seeing the man who had led him to the Lord. As Enoch reached his hand out to shake Elam's hand, Elam very formally stated: "Enoch, I have something to say to you."

Enoch was hesitant, yet patient: "Speak on, my friend."

"Enoch," his neighbor struggled to say, "I have come to apologize." Enoch was somewhat surprised by Elam's words. Before Enoch could respond, Elam uncharacteristically kept talking. "I have judged you wrongly, and I want to say I am sorry for how I mistreated you the last time I was here. I have noticed a great change in Elihu since he has been back home," Elam struggled to say as a tear formed in his eye. "He's more tender toward people. He's more respectful toward me." Elam turned a moment toward his son. "When I asked my boy what had happened to him, he told me that he has a new heart since he trusted fully in the Lord. I could not accept that answer, my friend, because I did not know what he meant. All I knew was that you were filling his head with stories about a personal relationship with a living God."

Elam, who had probably never spoken so much at one time, took a quick breath and continued. "Then, I heard about your encounter with Arphaxad at the city gate. Let me tell you, my friend, everyone has been talking about your new-found power."

"It's God's power," Enoch finally managed to interrupt.

"Let me continue," Elam hastily added. "Yes, Enoch, I have finally begun to realize that maybe God's power is involved after all. What you did at the city gate, no man could do. But what really helped me believe that you really were sincerely trying to walk with God, was when I heard that you took Arphaxad home with you to nurse back to health. Only the love of God would cause a man to do that!"

Elam's words rang strangely in Arphaxad's ears. They brought tears to Enoch and Sarah's eyes. Then Elam concluded: "Please forgive me, my friend."

Enoch for once was speechless as he stepped over to hug his neighbor. "God bless you, Elam," Enoch struggled to say. "I certainly forgive you." With that burden off of his chest, Elam turned his eyes toward Arphaxad, who felt extremely uncomfortable as five sets of eyes gazed at him. In self-defense, Arphaxad closed his eyes. "How is he?" Elam quietly asked.

Enoch answered softly: "I wish he were better, Elam. All he can move is his head, and he still can't speak because of the neck wound."

"I am still astonished that you would bring your daughter's kidnapper home to nurse back to health."

"Like I told Sarah, Elam, I believe it's what God wants me to do. I just believe that God wants us to love our enemies, to bless them, to do good unto them, and to pray for them."

Elam struggled with Enoch's words. "Enoch, I don't think I have even loved my friends, much less my enemies." Elam started to weep as he confessed the great emptiness in his heart. "Enoch, I desperately want what Elihu has. I want the love and joy and peace that he has. Help me, Enoch, help me."

Right there, in front of Sarah, Elihu, Methuselah, and Arphaxad, Enoch and Elam unashamedly knelt together at one of the divans, and Enoch led Elam in a simple sinner's prayer. "Dear God, I am indeed a sinner, unworthy of Your love," Elam quietly repeated after Enoch. "I need to be cleansed by the blood of the coming Redeemer. I repent of my sins and turn toward You and You alone for my salvation. Please save me and give me the grace to walk with You day by day. Until the Redeemer comes, Amen!"

Elam prayed that short prayer with an earnestness and childlikeness that Enoch had never before seen. Then, as happened previously to the farmer's son, peace like a river flooded Elam's soul. Tears of joy flowed down his cheeks as he rose and hugged Enoch. Then, he turned and hugged his son, who was also crying. "I believe, son, I really believe," said Elam between tears.

Sarah, too, was deeply moved by Elam's conversion. Perhaps God did have a purpose in bringing that miserable thug into her home. Perhaps God truly was working in Enoch's life in a very special way to turn people to God.

Meanwhile, Methuselah had mixed feelings. On the one hand, he was thrilled to see Elam reunited in friendship with his father. But on the other hand, it seemed like such a steep price for Elam to pay to be restored to Enoch's friendship. All of the talk about being a sinner and repentance still seemed a little foreign, and more than a little unnecessary, to the thirteen-year-old unbeliever.

Finally, Arphaxad, more than anyone, was struggling to understand what he saw. For the very first time, Arphaxad entertained the thought that perhaps Enoch was sincere.

## Chapter Eighteen

# Miracle

Elihu returned to live at Enoch's homestead, with his father's blessing. After his salvation, Elam came to realize that God had called Elihu to be a shepherd, not a farmer. Besides, Elam had other sons to help with his farm, while Enoch really needed Elihu's assistance. Elam was very grateful that he could help his new-found spiritual brother in any way.

Elihu was like another son to Sarah, always unfailingly polite and helpful. Elihu had a true shepherd's heart and was drawn to Arphaxad, still bedridden and unable to speak. Elihu adopted the thug as his special project, taking care of his food and bedding, much to the relief of the overworked, overwrought Sarah. The usually quiet Elihu, finding himself with a captive audience, began to tell him about farming and shepherding. At first, Arphaxad resented the storytelling, but as the days passed into weeks, he started to appreciate Elihu's storytelling as a relief from the tedious ways of the country folk.

More than anyone else, Methuselah loved to have Elihu around. He was the brother that Methuselah never had. Although Elihu was at times a little bit too spiritual for Methuselah's taste, nonetheless, Methuselah loved having the company of another young man around the homestead and in the fields.

Enoch continued to pray for his expanded family. He praised God that he, his wife, and Elihu were believers. He praised God that Elihu, an active, growing believer, was in his household as a role model and good influence upon Methuselah. Enoch prayed for his son every day, praying that Methuselah would trust in the coming Redeemer as his Savior, and that he would accept God's call upon their lives.

One beautiful fall morning, Enoch was down by the stream, praying as usual for the needs of his family, praising God for His beautiful creation, and thanking God for the mighty blessings which God had bestowed upon him and upon his family. That quiet spot beside the stream, so restful, peaceful, and meditative, was where Enoch seemed to walk most closely with the Lord.

As Enoch raised his eyes and voice to Heaven and spoke out loud -- "I love You, Lord!" -- Enoch heard a familiar voice on the other side of the stream reply, "I love you, Enoch!" Enoch swiveled his head and stared in astonishment as the Lord appeared on the other side of the stream. Enoch, immediately reminded of his first sight of the Lord across the River of Life in the Garden of Eden, prostrated himself and proclaimed: "My Lord and my God!"

The vision of the Lord calmly spoke again: "Arise, My son! It is nigh time for you to go and to preach to other cities, other regions, as I have earlier called and commanded you to do."

Enoch slowly arose. With shaking knees and voice, he asked his Lord: "Where shall I go, and who shall go with me, my Lord?"

God was so patient and peaceful as He responded: "I shall raise up a traveling companion for you, Enoch."

"Who will it be, Lord? Will it be Elihu? or Methuselah?"

"I shall reveal it to you soon, My son," God replied. "The two of you must journey to the City of Gom and even to the City of Cain, and you must tell them what you have heard and seen of Me."

"When will that be, Lord?"

"When I raise up your traveling companion."

"Be it unto me according to Thy word," Enoch humbly said as the vision of the Lord disappeared.

Enoch returned from the stream to the house and shared his vision with the family during lunchtime. Sarah and Elihu were both excited about God's appearing to Enoch right there at the homestead. Elihu excitedly offered to take care of the sheep while Enoch was away preaching.

Sarah's heart was as prepared as a wife's heart could be at the imminent departure of her husband. She was confident that the best thing she could do as a wife was to let her husband walk with God, no matter where He led him.

Methuselah was disappointed again. He loved being in the hills with his father and sheep. Why did God want to rob him of his greatest joy? Methuselah also was fearful that perhaps God would raise up Elihu as Enoch's traveling companion. An even more unsettling thought occurred to Methuselah: "Perhaps, God wants me to travel with Dad." The young lad was torn by his desire to be with his dad and by his great distaste for his father's mission to preach. "And what would happen to Mom if Dad and I went off together?" Methuselah was truly disturbed by Enoch's latest proclamation.

Arphaxad was amazed. He had never known anyone to speak of such a personal encounter with the hitherto unknown God. He had stopped trying to convince himself that Enoch was hypocritical, instead concluding that Enoch was crazy. But Arphaxad admitted to himself that Enoch's craziness brought great peace into Enoch's own life and in the lives of others around him.

That evening after supper Enoch and his family had family devotions around the eating table. Arphaxad, bedridden, lay in the bed at the other end of the common room. Enoch told the story he had heard from Adam about how Cain's murder of Abel was such a crushing blow to Eve.

Enoch explained how Abel was lost to death and Cain was lost to sin. Enoch explained how Adam and Eve lost hope that the Redeemer would ever come, lost hope that the penalty for their sins would ever be paid for, lost hope that they would ever see God again.

Methuselah realized that hope was missing in his heart. Enoch concluded his story with Adam's remark that "a man without hope is already dead."

Then Enoch prayed. He prayed much as he did the night Elihu was saved. He hoped and prayed that his son would be converted. "Dear God, be merciful to me a sinner. Forgive my iniquities, O God. Forgive the iniquities of my wife and my son. Forgive the iniquities of Elihu and the iniquities of Arphaxad."

As Enoch prayed, he heard a muffled sound, like a soft sob, from within the room. He continued to pray: "O God, reprove the world of sin and of righteousness and of judgment."

Enoch could feel the Spirit of God descend upon the room as he continued: "God, the heart of man truly is deceitful above all things, and desperately wicked. Open up the heart, Lord, of any of us who resist Your Spirit."

The muffled sob was heard again as Enoch continued to pray: "Let each one of us recognize our sinfulness and our need to be cleansed by the blood of the Lamb, by the blood of the coming Redeemer."

The unction of the Holy Spirit was mighty as Enoch concluded his prayer: "If any of us tonight does not believe in You, Lord, if any of us tonight does not look forward to the blessed hope and glorious appearing of our Redeemer, then Lord, I pray, I beseech You, that You fill that heart with more grace that he might believe."

The muffled sob was heard again. All eyes remained closed, out of respect to the struggling soul, whoever he was, who was being mightily convicted by the Spirit of God. Again, a sob was heard, then a grunt, as the voice struggled to speak through the tears.

Finally, the voice was able to speak, softly, in a whisper, barely audible in the room: "I believe." Again, the whispering voice spoke a little more strongly: "I believe." All eyes at the table turned toward the other end of the room as the bedridden Arphaxad whispered for the third time: "I believe."

## Chapter Nineteen

# Arphaxad's Boyhood

The miracle of Arphaxad's spiritual healing was soon followed by the miracle of his physical healing. By the next morning, Arphaxad was able to sit up and whisper a conversation. Within a week he was slowly walking about the homestead with the help of a staff.

Arphaxad had never before been happy; but now, his heart was filled with joy. Remarkably, he shared his joy with his fellow believers. Enoch, Sarah, and Elihu were all delighted by the cheerful and talkative patient, who himself delighted in constantly praising the Lord.

Only Methuselah failed to share in the joyous mood. He was still too hurt by the loss of Crista to forgive Arphaxad, and it just did not seem right to him that such a wicked, evil man could be converted.

But converted Arphaxad was. He told his new brothers and sister that his life had always been characterized by violence, but that he now knew a peace that passeth understanding.

Over a period of several days Arphaxad told the story of his previous life, a life brutally fascinating to his shocked listeners. Even Enoch, who knew more of the ways of the world than anyone else in his family, was shocked at many of the tales of Arphaxad. "My father was a blacksmith in the City of Cain. He was a big man, a giant man, a proud man. One day, when I was only five years old, my mother, a beautiful, dark-haired woman only twenty-five years old, came home and announced to my father that she had been selected to become a priestess for the Tower."

Enoch's mind went back to that tall tower with the temple on top that he had seen when riding through the City of Cain. He listened intently as Arphaxad continued: "My father was in shock. He loved my mother. He begged and pleaded with her to stay at home. But mother was adamant, seemingly bewitched or spellbound. She constantly repeated 'The High Priest Cain himself has selected me.'"

At the mention of that name, Enoch's mind raced back to the story told to him by Adam about Adam's two sons. Enoch was entranced as Arphaxad continued to talk. "Mother left that very night to live with the other priestesses in a large house next to Cain's mansion. There, in that house, she worshipped the large ebony cow which Cain had built with his own hands." Enoch and Sarah looked quickly at each other as Arphaxad mentioned the large ebony cow. Thoughts of Zaava passed through their minds.

Arphaxad continued: "In Cain's mansion, many men come to worship the cow. A man would pay something to one of Cain's eunuchs. Then the man would bow down to worship the large ebony cow. Finally, one of the priestesses would take the man off to one of the private chambers." Sarah was shocked at Arphaxad's story. She could not help but think what went on in Zaava's chamber.

"My father kept pleading with my mother. He even went to appeal to Cain to please let his wife return home. Cain just laughed at my proud, hurting father. Cain told my father that his wife had been called to a higher profession than just being the wife of a common blacksmith. Cain told my father that he should be honored that the high priest himself had called his wife to be a priestess."

Enoch was sickened by the image of the poor, desperate husband. "What did your father do, Arphaxad?"

Arphaxad cried. "I was only five, but I remember it all. I come home one day and found my father in the livery stable. He had hung himself from one of the rafters."

Sarah cried, too. So did Elihu. Arphaxad continued to unburden his heart. "That was when I learned to hate God, if there was a God. He had stolen my mother, killed my father, and stolen my childhood."

"What happened to you then?" asked an incredulous Elihu.

"Cain confiscated my father's home and blacksmith shop. He placed one of his priests in charge of the blacksmith shop. That's where the railing around the Tower was built."

A wounded look appeared in the ex-thug's eyes. "The priest in charge of the blacksmith shop was very cruel to me. He whipped me all the time. But I had nowhere to go. I rarely saw my mother, who lost interest in me as she progressed through the rites of the priestesshood. When I was thirteen, I was as tall and as strong as most grown men. One day the priest who terrorized my life whipped my severely with his whip. I became so angry that I hit him when he turned his back. Then I took his whip and strangled him to death. Then I ran away."

Arphaxad stopped. He pondered what he had just said, then he continued: "I was always so proud of my first murder. Now, I'm sorry for killing him. And I'm sorry for killing all of the other people I have murdered." Arphaxad stopped again, cried, and asked God to forgive him.

Enoch's heart was touched. "My brother, it is a good thing to ask God's forgiveness, but God has already forgiven you of all your sins."

"All of them?" Arphaxad cried like a poor, little child.

"Yes, all of them, my dear brother."

But Arphaxad was not completely consoled. "But think of the many lives and families I have ruined!" He wept bitterly.

Enoch reached up and put his arm around Arphaxad's shoulders. "Only a true child of God would weep bitterly over his sins. God will surely give you an opportunity to make restitution to all of those families."

"Oh, Enoch," Arphaxad sobbed, "I hope so. And I do want to make it up to everybody. But I have been to so many places and hurt so many people. How can I ever make it up to all of them?"

Enoch contemplated Arphaxad's predicament for a moment. Then Enoch abruptly slapped his own forehead. "Of course!" he shouted.

"Of course what?" Arphaxad asked.

"I'll go with you, my brother, when you make restitution for all of your offenses against people."

"You mean that you would do that for me?" a grateful Arphaxad asked.

Enoch smiled. "Of course, Arphaxad. I think God wants me to be your traveling companion."

## Chapter Twenty

# Arphaxad's Story Continued

Enoch's revelation of who would be his traveling companion stunned everyone at Enoch's homestead. Sarah chided her husband: "Dear, I don't think anyone would ever accept you and Arphaxad as an evangelistic team. So many people, including your own family, have been so terribly hurt by Arphaxad in the past. Although he has been converted, I don't think many people will accept him -- or you with him."

"But don't you see, Sarah? Only God could raise up Arphaxad and Enoch. God must be in it."

"Your faith, Enoch, is once again ahead of mine."

"But, dear, there are certain advantages to Arphaxad being my traveling companion."

"Like what?" demanded Sarah.

"My traveling companion won't be Methuselah or Elihu."

Sarah pondered Enoch's words for a moment. "You somehow find the right thing to say to assuage me, Enoch, but I still am dubious about the team of Enoch and Arphaxad."

"Let's just trust God in this matter, dear."

"I certainly will, dear, because I don't trust you." With those concluding words, Sarah settled the matter in her mind.

To Enoch's surprise, Methuselah's reaction to Enoch's revelation was much more enthusiastic. Methuselah had finally accepted that God had called his father to be a traveling preacher, so now Methuselah was just relieved that God had not called him -- or Elihu -- to be his father's traveling companion. "At least Elihu and I can stay home together and tend the sheep, Dad!"

Elihu was likewise gladdened at Enoch's revelation. "Sir, ever since Arphaxad entered your household, I have taken a special interest in him. In my shy, humble, limited way, I tried to be a friend to Arphaxad, to interest him in the ways of the country and in the ways of God. That God would see fit to use my friend to tell others about God, well, I am so honored, sir."

Enoch was so encouraged by the response of his family that even Enoch himself started to lose most of his apprehension about traveling with the ex-thug. As for Arphaxad, he just focused on his inexperience at being a blessing to people instead of being a curse. As Arphaxad continued to recuperate, he continued to share details of his life.

"After I ran away from the City of Cain, I lived off the land for several years. One day I heard that my mother had accidentally gotten pregnant. When the child was born, she gave the baby, a little boy, to the high priest."

Sarah was intrigued, and somewhat frightened, that Arphaxad had a brother. "What did Cain want the baby boy for?"

"You mean that you have never heard, Sarah?"

"No, I haven't."

"Well, I guess it's OK to tell you. Cain has commanded that the first-born child of every priestess in his priestess house be sacrificed to the Great Ebony Cow."

Sarah and the others gasped as Arphaxad continued to explain. "Cain would leave the child with the mother for eight days, just long enough for the mother to develop a strong maternal bond with the infant. Then the mother would have to give up her child to Cain as proof of her undying devotion to Cain and the Great Ebony Cow. Then Cain would climb the Tower. While more priests and priestesses would start the fire in the flaming pit below, and while other priests and priestesses would play loud, sensuous music, Cain would walk to the edge of the west platform extending from the temple. After offering the child to his god, he would throw the infant away from the temple, down, down, down, until it landed in the flaming pit below."

Moans escaped from everybody's mouth. Sarah almost gagged. But Arphaxad continued his grisly story. "I hated God, if there was a God, even more for killing my brother. I became like a wounded wild beast. For years I terrorized the countryside, maiming and killing people in a furious revenge over the death of my brother."

Arphaxad's face became contorted with a mixture of grief and fury as he continued his story. "Then, when I was twenty, I heard that my mother had had another child."

Sarah hesitated to ask: "Was that child murdered, too?"

"No, Sarah, the second and all subsequent children born to priestesses are raised in the priestess house annex. Baby girls are raised up to be priestesses and baby boys are raised up to be eunuchs."

Enoch, Methuselah, and Elihu flinched as Arphaxad continued. "My sister grew up to be a beautiful young lady, but her beauty was only skin deep. Her heart was as corrupt as the heart of Cain. She was selected by Cain to become a high priestess. Only the most beautiful and most corrupt priestesses are so honored. At age eighteen she moved into Cain's own mansion. There he instructed her into the deepest mysteries and the greatest perversities known to man."

"What do high priestesses do?" Sarah again hesitantly asked.

"They are trained to spread the cult of the Great Ebony Cow."

Enoch was intrigued. "Just what is Cain's obsession with cows?"

Arphaxad thought for a moment, then replied: "I never thought about it before. But now that I am saved and have heard you tell the Words of God about Adam and Eve and Cain and Abel, perhaps it makes sense. Cain had offered to God the wrong sacrifice when both he and his brother Abel offered sacrifices to God. Cain offered the works of his own hands, while Abel offered in obedience to God an animal sacrifice. God's rebuke to Cain led to Abel's murder."

As Arphaxad had a passing thought of some of the people that he himself had murdered, Enoch quickly encouraged him, "Go on."

"Perhaps Cain established the worship of animals as some sort of twisted revenge against God for God's judgment upon Cain after the murder of Abel. Perhaps Cain wanted to get people to worship the creature more than the Creator. Cain uses high priestesses from his mansion to celebrate this perverted religion. For the last hundred years or so, Cain has spread this foul religion by sending high priestesses across the countryside."

"How does he do that?"

"He usually marries off a young high priestess to some unsuspecting country bumpkin who is either visiting or getting an education in the City of Cain."

"Do the husbands know what their wives are up to?" queried Enoch.

"Not usually. Cain is very clever. He calls these young high priestesses his own daughters. He offers a very ample dowry to these ambitious young men, who agree to marry and settle as a businessman in a city that Cain chooses."

"Has Cain married off your sister?" Sarah again hesitantly asked.

"Yes, he has, about six years ago."

"What city did she move to?"

"The City of Gom."

## Chapter Twenty-one

# Arphaxad's Startling Revelation

The room was silent as each listener tried to absorb Arphaxad's startling revelation. Slowly, beams of enlightenment, or rather beams of darkness, flashed in each face, stunning the listeners. Finally, Sarah blurted out: "You mean --"

"Yes," Arphaxad replied, completing Sarah's sentence, "Zaava is my sister."

Even though they had guessed it, each listener was also stunned by Arphaxad's words. A whirlwind of thoughts spun around the room. Finally, Enoch was able to ask: "Does Tubal know?"

"About Zaava and me? Of course not. Tubal is a fool. All he is interested in is making money. He was just a poor but ambitious country bumpkin when he met Zaava in the City of Cain. He fell in love with the dowry more than anything else. He saw in Zaava a shortcut to riches."

Enoch's heart ached for his old childhood friend, fearful of the price which he had paid for riches. "Does Tubal know about Zaava being a high priestess?"

"Oh, he knows a little bit, but not much. And I don't think he wants to know. For Tubal, ignorance is bliss."

"How far has Zaava gone in the fiendish rites of her cow cult?"

"Oh, Zaava is taking her time, slowly building up her religion. Already she offers herself regularly to numerous men in the city, for a donation, of course."

Sarah winced inside. "What does she want from these poor, beguiled men?"

"First, she wants their loyalty. Men such as Lalomar are her slaves."

Enoch now winced, tracing in his mind how Tubal's sin of greed had now led to Lalomar's corruption. "What does Zaava want to do with those donations?"

"Her goal is to build a temple in the City of Gom."

"Oh, no!" screamed Sarah.

Arphaxad ignored Sarah's scream. "Zaava is ambitious, and in her own mind, unbeatable. She will not let anyone stop her, not Tubal, not Enoch."

"God can stop her, my brother," Enoch insisted.

"Only God can." The ex-thug was quiet for a moment. "Enoch, did you ever wonder why Tubal was always gone when my friends and I showed up?"

"Were you working for Tubal?" Enoch asked incredulously.

"Of course not. Tubal is a legitimate businessman. No, my sister used my special skills to advance her designs. And she used that puny little Lalomar to send messages to me."

Enoch's mouth suddenly became bitter as Arphaxad unraveled the many threads of Zaava's scheme. "You did not know it, Enoch, but that day last year when you came to the city, Lalomar reported your arrival to Zaava. Zaava then instructed me to kill you." The ex-thug then wept as he thought of his nearly fatal success. "Please forgive me, Enoch!"

Enoch was moved by Arphaxad's story, and even more so by his tender request for forgiveness. "Of course, my brother, as God has forgiven you, so do I."

Arphaxad continued to weep as he further confessed: "It was my own perverted, spontaneous idea to kidnap your daughter Crista." The repentant ex-thug just broke down and bawled.

Sarah sobbed. So did Enoch and Elihu. Each of them could not find words to express their grief and their forgiveness to Arphaxad. But Methuselah's heart was not tender, his mouth not quiet. "What did you do with my sister?" Methuselah demanded.

Arphaxad lowered his eyes, obviously deeply wounded by his own sin and by the young lad's stinging question. "I -- I -- I --"

"Answer me now, Arphaxad!" Methuselah screamed out.

Before Enoch or Sarah could react to Methuselah's understandable but impolite impertinence, Arphaxad answered: "I sold her at the slave market in the City of Cain."

Everyone's heart sank at Arphaxad's startling revelation. Again, only Methuselah had the anger to ask: "Whom did you sell her to?"

Once again, Arphaxad answered quickly: "I sold her to a ship captain named Captain Blackheart."

Sarah and Enoch were speechless as Methuselah pressed on: "Where is my sister now?"

"I don't know, young lad. I don't know. Captain Blackheart is a slave trader. He could have taken Crista almost anywhere in the world."

Methuselah was outraged. He stormed out of the room. The ex-thug felt awful. Enoch, still shocked and grieved at Arphaxad's revelations, managed to walk over to Arphaxad and give him a hug. "It's all right, my brother, it's all right."

"No, it's not," Arphaxad cried. "You will probably never see your daughter again, all because of me."

"No, Arphaxad," Enoch earnestly replied. "You're wrong. I now see how God used the kidnapping of Crista to bring me to God, and to bring Elihu to God, and yes, even you to God. You meant it for evil, but God used it for good."

"Oh, Enoch, maybe you are right. But what about Crista? You will never see her again."

"No, my brother, I shall certainly see her again."

"How can you be so sure?"

"God told me."

# Part Two

# Journey to the City of Cain

**701 A.C.**

## Chapter Twenty-two

# Odd Couple in Gom

Arphaxad's physical recovery and spiritual development were remarkable. Day after day Enoch shared with him the Words of God and the insights which God had given to the prophet of God.

Arphaxad was chomping at the bit to start his new, God-ordained role as Enoch's traveling companion. He was burdened to reach as many people as possible with his heartfelt apology and his heart-warming testimony of God's marvelous salvation. Sarah was surprised at herself that she had regrets that one day Arphaxad would be leaving the homestead; the ex-thug's enthusiasm for life in general and for spiritual matters was infectious and would be sorely missed.

The day Sarah dreaded finally came. Enoch announced one morning that he and Arphaxad would make their long-awaited trip to the City of Gom and even beyond. Enoch asked Methuselah and Elihu to take extra care of Sarah in his absence, and to let Sarah do all of the cooking. After Sarah baked a batch of biscuits and everyone had a time of prayer, tearful good-byes and I'll-see-you-soons were shared. As the two traveling companions walked to the top of the hill and waved back to the family they were leaving behind, Sarah couldn't help but wonder: "Will I ever see Enoch again?"

Enoch and Arphaxad had a joyous time talking as they walked toward the City of Gom. As Enoch pointed out the varieties of trees waving to them as they passed by, Arphaxad commented: "I never used to be interested in God's creation. I can't believe all that I have missed. I spent way too much time in the cities."

"Are you known in many cities, Arphaxad?" Enoch queried.

"Ah, my brother," the ex-thug replied, "the name of Arphaxad is known and feared throughout the land. Now, I want the name of the Lord to be known and feared throughout the land." Enoch was thrilled with his companion. God had indeed selected the perfect traveling companion for the prophet of God.

The entrance of Enoch and Arphaxad -- together -- into the City of Gom was a momentous occasion. All activity ceased in the marketplace as people stared at the odd couple, who just calmly ignored the gawking, finger-pointing, whispering merchants and customers. One of the merchants, Lalomar, recovered himself sufficiently to scurry to Zaava's house.

Meanwhile, Enoch and Arphaxad stopped to visit Ludim and Perna. Ludim almost had another heart attack when he saw Arphaxad walk into his blacksmith shop, then almost had still another one when he saw Enoch walk in smiling right behind the hitherto thug. As Ludim stood gawking, Enoch calmly introduced his new brother. Ludim looked at Enoch, then looked at Arphaxad, then looked at Enoch again. "Glory be!" the blacksmith bellowed. Ludim stepped forward and gave Arphaxad one of his incredible bearhugs, which caused the still somewhat tender ex-thug a considerable amount of pain, which Ludim completely ignored. "Wait until Perna hears this!" Ludim shouted, as he led the two men toward the house. As the men neared the front door of the house, Ludim had a sudden inspiration. "Let's surprise Perna."

"Are you sure?" Arphaxad asked quizzically.

"Ah, sure, Perna's heart is in good shape. Arphaxad, you knock on the door while Enoch and I hide behind this bush."

The ex-thug meekly complied. Knock-knock. As Arphaxad heard someone coming to answer the door, a silly grin crept across his face. As the door opened, the hulking ex-thug made every attempt to look harmless, but to no avail. As soon as Perna gazed upward to look into Arphaxad's face, a pleasant smile erupted into a look of terror, followed immediately by a scream: "LUDIM!"

"Yes, dear?" Ludim calmly asked as he stepped out from behind the bush. Perna rushed by the startled visitor into the waiting arms of her laughing husband. "Ludim, that's Arphaxad!"

"Oh, yes, dear, we have met before."

"What's he doing on my front porch?" Perna asked with consternation and puzzlement as her husband kept laughing.

"Why, Perna, Arphaxad is now a brother in the Lord."

Perna looked up at Arphaxad, whose grin became even sillier. Then Enoch stepped out from behind the bush and said to a still confused Perna, "It's true, Perna. God has saved Arphaxad's soul."

Perna looked once again at all three men, then turned toward Ludim. "You're not getting any dinner," she said playfully as she hustled the three hungry men into her house. All four of them helped to put dinner on while Arphaxad excitedly told his testimony to the dear couple. After saying the blessing over the food and praising God for the new believer, Ludim asked: "What are you two going to do here in the City of Gom?"

Enoch simply replied: "God has commanded me and my traveling companion to preach here in the City of Gom and in the other cities along the road, even unto the City of Cain."

"I must say, my friend," Ludim observed, "you two certainly are ambitious."

"No," Enoch explained, "God is ambitious."

"God is certainly using you in a remarkable way, Enoch, and you, too, Arphaxad. You can be sure of my continued prayers for you."

As they continued to eat, Enoch asked: "Whatever happened to that little girl Martha?"

"She's over at a friend's house this afternoon."

"You mean that she is still here in Gom?"

"Oh, yes," replied Perna. "We found out from her that she is an orphan." Before Perna could say another word, she noticed that a tear was streaking down Arphaxad's cheek.

"Is Martha the little girl I threatened to murder when I was last here in Gom?"

Perna's heart almost broke for the big ex-thug. "Yes, Arphaxad, Martha is quite all right. She is living with us now. Really, Ludim must thank you for bringing that little ray of sunlight into our lives."

"I must apologize to Martha for how I mistreated her."

"Oh, there will be plenty of time for that, Arphaxad."

Just then, Perna asked: "What's that I hear outside?"

## Chapter Twenty-three

# Preaching at Gom

Ludim went to the front window to look outside. There, milling in the street, was a large crowd of city dwellers. "Enoch, come look at this."

Enoch arose from the table and peeked out the window. "Are they up to mischief?"

"Probably not," Ludim replied. "The city has been very good and very quiet since your last trip to the city. Your victory over Arphaxad really took some wind out of the corruption."

"Then what are all those people doing out there?"

"They are probably as startled as Perna and I were to see you and Arphaxad together."

"Well then," Enoch continued, "let's not disappoint them." Then Enoch turned toward Arphaxad and announced: "This is it, my brother. Let's go and walk up to the city gate."

Arphaxad was not eager to leave Perna's biscuits, but he got up and looked out the window. "Enoch, do your really think I can speak in front of a big crowd like that?"

"You've done it before, my brother."

"Ah, that was different, Enoch. I was a thug then, full of pride."

Enoch calmly replied: "Now you are full of God."

Arphaxad gulped, then said: "Let's go!"

Ludim said a quick prayer for the two travelers, who then stepped out on the front porch.

"That's Enoch, for sure," one city dweller yelled out.

"Yeah," another city dweller replied, "but are you sure the other one is Arphaxad?"

"Looks like him, although I have never seen Arphaxad cleaned up."

The crowd parted for the two travelers as they walked out onto the street and toward the marketplace. The crowd grew bigger as word spread instantly across the city that Enoch and Arphaxad were making their way to the city gate.

As the procession neared the city gate, Enoch saw Tubal and Zaava and Enoch's brother Aram just ahead. Enoch said hello to his old friend Tubal, who had always conveniently disappeared in times past whenever Arphaxad came to town. Enoch even gave his brother Aram a quick handshake as they passed.

Arphaxad, with a ridiculously cheerful and sunny disposition, said hello to his sister. Zaava, rarely at a loss for words, was utterly stunned. She had never before seen her brother cleaned up or in a cheerful mood. Her mind could not accept the obvious -- Arphaxad was now a believer in God.

Enoch and Arphaxad made their way up the steps to the east platform. There was no need for theatrics from Enoch's staff of God. The odd couple, standing together on the east platform, held the rapt attention of the entire city.

As was to become their practice, the taller, broader Arphaxad spoke first. All eyes were upon the ex-thug as he started to speak: "People of Gom, I have returned to your city. But I have a new message for you. No longer do I bring you a message of hatred and fear. Now I bring you a message of love and peace."

The gathered multitude began to buzz over the strange words emanating from the thug's mouth. "I am no longer a thug. I have repented of my sins. I have repented of my evil past. God has saved me from my sins. I am now a child of God."

Zaava became furious. "What awful thing has happened to my brother?"

Arphaxad explained the question that arose in so many minds. "After I was struck down by Enoch at this very spot so many months ago, I almost died. Only by the great compassion and tenderness of Enoch and his family, am I even alive and standing before you today."

Zaava cursed Enoch: "Ah, it's you, Sheep Man, who has done this terrible thing to my brother."

Arphaxad continued: "I was nursed back to health at Enoch's homestead. At first I was terrified of being in the house of a man I had brutally beaten up and almost murdered. But instead of receiving wrath for wrath, I received love and joy and peace."

Zaava's face contorted the words love and joy and peace. Arphaxad, who had now overcome all hesitation at speaking to the crowd, carried on. "At first I was skeptical of Enoch and his family, as many of you may be. I thought Enoch was a hypocrite. I did not believe his wild tales of walking with God."

Zaava spit on the ground and hissed at Enoch as Arphaxad spoke. "But for weeks I saw Enoch in his home, so loving and kind towards his wife, his son, his friends, and yes, even me, his enemy."

Zaava continued to mutter to herself: "You are still my enemy, Sheep Man."

Arphaxad finally concluded his speech: "I ask two things of you, people of Gom. First, please forgive me for all the harm I have done to you."

Zaava muttered to no one in particular: "I will never forgive you, my brother, for becoming a follower of God."

Then Arphaxad finished: "And second, please listen to Enoch, a man who has walked with God."

All eyes turned toward Enoch, who held the staff of God in his right hand. All movement in the multitude ceased as the prophet of God began to speak. "People of Gom, I bring you a message of hope today. If God can save a wretch like me, if God can save a wretch like Arphaxad, then God could save each and every one of you who hears my voice today."

Enoch's opening words sounded strange in many ears, especially in the ears of Enoch's brother Aram. "What do I need to be saved from? I'm healthy. I've got a good job with Tubal."

Enoch's voice grew stronger. "I searched for God for many months. I was a broken and defeated man, constantly aware of my loneliness and my mortality. I kept searching for God until God found me. You can find God, too."

Aram was insolent. "Who needs God? I've got myself."

Enoch took a breath before he continued. "God's message of love and hope is tempered with justice. God is a holy God Who cannot stand sin. Each person must recognize that he is a sinner who falls short of the glory of God. Each person must admit that he needs the coming Redeemer."

Aram became infuriated with his fanatical brother. "Don't call me a sinner!" Aram spat.

Even from a distance, Enoch could see the fury in his brother's face. But Enoch was not dismayed and kept right on preaching. "God wants each of you to trust in the blood of the coming Redeemer, to repent of your sinful ways, and to walk with God every day."

"I would rather die first!" Aram concluded in his mind.

Then Enoch concluded: "My heart aches for you, people of Gom. Turn from your wicked ways and avoid the wrath to come. God has saved me from my sins. He has saved Arphaxad from his sins. God wants to save you today. Turn back to God today."

The crowd was respectful. Even Zaava remained quiet as she plotted in her mind how to rid the Earth of these two religious nuts. But no one in the crowd responded to Enoch's appeal. He was momentarily disappointed until he remembered that God only called him to preach; the results were up to God.

The crowd dispersed. They still did not like Enoch, but they now had a new respect for him. Even Zaava had more respect for Enoch, as one respects a deadly viper. As she walked back to her home, she commanded Aram to find out what Enoch's plans were. Then she told her husband: "As soon as we discover Enoch's plans, let us take a trip to see my father Cain. He will tell us what to do with the Sheep Man and my lamebrained brother."

## Chapter Twenty-four

# On the Road

Aram was friendly as Enoch and Arphaxad walked by. Aram, oozing familial concern, filled his brother in on family news. Enoch was happy to hear any news about his family, but Arphaxad merely watched Aram with a cynical eye. When Aram asked his brother "And so what are your plans, Enoch?", Arphaxad quickly interjected: "Aram, you can tell my sister Zaava that Enoch and I shall travel from city to city to preach, even unto the City of Cain."

Aram turned and snarled at Arphaxad, then responded: "Mind your own business, thug!" Enoch did not know what to think of the exchange. He said a friendly good-bye to his brother, then walked out of the north gate with Arphaxad, by which time Aram was already at Zaava's house. "It's a good thing you've got me along, Enoch," Arphaxad dryly observed.

The daily walk northward to the next city was wonderful for Enoch and Arphaxad. Enoch shared even more details of Adam and Eve, of the wilderness, of Enoch's confrontation with Satan, of the cherubim, of the Garden of Eden, and finally of God Himself. Arphaxad's lively mind lapped up the Words of God like a thirsty dog laps up water.

Enoch was likewise fascinated by Arphaxad's knowledge of the countryside, of the various cities, and especially of the High Priest Cain. The prophet of God was all ears as Arphaxad explained the source of Cain's power and wickedness: "Cain was always rebellious against God. From the beginning, he wanted to offer sacrifices to God his own way, not God's way."

"Cain was extremely selfish. He did not care for the feelings of others. He did not care that his mother would be crushed by his brother's death. Cain's motto has always been: 'Am I my brother's keeper?'"

"Enoch, there can be great power in rebellion and selfishness. Such rebels and self-willed persons open themselves up to the power of Satan, the original rebel and self-willed one. And we both know how subtle and powerful the Evil One is."

"But Cain believes that he has power even beyond the Evil One. After he murdered Abel, Cain was afraid that either God or men would kill him. Though God cursed Cain in other respects, in this one respect God blessed Cain in a most remarkable way."

"The Lord said unto Cain, 'Whosoever slayeth Cain, vengeance shall be taken on him sevenfold.' And the Lord God set a mark upon Cain."

Arphaxad finally took a breath, and Enoch questioned: "How does Cain derive power from the mark of Cain?"

"My brother," Arphaxad replied, "Cain believes that he will never die. He believes that God, Who could have struck him dead after he killed Abel, will not kill him. Cain believes that men are afraid, because of God's curse, to kill him. So Cain feels that he is invincible. He derives great power from that illusion."

"Cain will die someday in his sins, Arphaxad," Enoch corrected.

"Yes, you know that, and now I know that. But believe me, Enoch, Cain has a lot of people fooled into believing otherwise."

"How can people be so foolish?" Enoch quizzed.

"It's not hard to imagine," Arphaxad answered. "First of all, it is obvious that Cain has not yet died. That's one thing in his favor. Second, Cain appeals to the rebellion and selfishness found in the heart of man. And third, Cain uses, with great effect as a sign of power, the mark of God upon his forehead. He tells people that the mark of Cain is a sign of his special anointing. The many priests and priestesses are commanded to kiss the mark of Cain at least once a year as a sign of their continued submission and devotion to him."

"That's sick!" the prophet of God said with disgust. As the two walked on for a minute, Enoch pondered all that he heard about the "invincible" Cain. Then Enoch asked: "I wonder what it is like dealing with a man who feels like he will never die."

"Let me tell you, Enoch, Cain is a very commanding personality. I would hate to face him some day as an adversary."

"One day we shall, my friend."

"But I'm not ready, Enoch."

"Neither am I, Arphaxad, neither am I. But we have a long way to go before we reach the City of Cain. As for now, we must walk and wait for God to strengthen us."

Arphaxad laughed: "I'm afraid that waiting was never one of my strong points, Enoch."

"Me, too," Enoch chuckled. "But I have a feeling that tribulation worketh patience, and that you and I will be learning a lot of patience soon."

"Thanks for the encouragement," Arphaxad replied sarcastically.

"Really, Arphaxad, we must learn to wait on God. They that wait upon the Lord shall renew their strength. They shall mount up with wings as eagles. That's what I want!" Enoch boldly said. "I want to wait upon the Lord and mount up with wings as eagles." Enoch looked up into the sky and repeated: "Mount up with wings as eagles."

## Chapter Twenty-five

# Cain

Tubal prepared his coach and fastest team of horses for the long trip to the City of Cain. Tubal left his servant in charge of the household as Tubal, Aram, Zaava, and Zaava's maid left for the journey to the City of Cain. Tubal pushed the horses very hard and covered the four hundred and fifty miles in four days.

Reaction to the City of Cain varied among the passengers. Zaava was thrilled to be home, back home in the center of civilization, and even more importantly, the center of culture. How she despised the doltish city dwellers in the City of Gom.

Aram was still young and very fascinated by the sights and sounds of the world's largest city. He was also excited about the prospect of meeting High Priest Cain for the first time.

Tubal's reaction was vastly different. He was a pure businessman, calculating what could be gained from the news which he bore. But Tubal never relished an audience with Cain, who demanded perfect obedience, something which the independent-minded Tubal could give to no man. Yet, Cain was useful to Tubal, and Tubal was useful to Cain.

Aram still marveled at all of the beautiful buildings as they rode through the south gate. Aram had never been to school and was fascinated by the magnificent edifices of learning sprinkled throughout the huge city. But there was no time for loitering. Tubal headed the coach directly to Cain's mansion.

The mansion was enormous, the largest house that Aram had ever seen. The mansion, plus the priestess house next door, covered an entire city block. Tubal, Zaava, and Aram jumped out of the coach at the main entrance. Zaava directed the butler, an old acquaintance of hers, to announce her arrival to Cain.

While their luggage was being unpacked, Tubal, Zaava, and Aram waited in the common room. Aram took the opportunity to examine the mammoth room, which was twice as long and twice as wide as the common room in Tubal's home. "Cain must truly be a great man!" Aram said to himself in awe.

In the south corner of the huge room was a gargatuan ebony cow, thirty feet high. At the base of the ebony cow was an oversized golden throne.

A balcony extended completely around the north, west, and east walls. From there, servants would be able to light the candles, thousands of candles, in the twenty crystal chandeliers which spread throughout the room. Aram was lost in counting the multitude of candles.

Meanwhile, Zaava was becoming impatient. Finally, Theron, the chief priest under Cain, appeared at the door leading to the rest of the house. "High Priestess Zaava," the oily Theron asked, "have you come to visit your dear, beloved mother?"

Zaava shot back: "I don't want to see that old hag. I must see Cain immediately. We have important news."

"I am afraid that that would be quite impossible, my dear Zaava," Theron sneered. "Our lord and master is attending to matters of the utmost importance."

"Get off it, Theron," Zaava hissed. "I'm telling you, Theron, our news is very important."

"I see, Lady Zaava," Theron said wickedly. "I shall arrange for you to meet with Cain, in exactly one hour." Then, with a lustful eye, Theron walked right up to Zaava and said: "But before you may visit the High Priest Cain, you must first be purified. Come with me to my private chamber and confess to me there."

Tubal was indignant. "Theron, we have no time for your silly religious ceremonies."

Theron spat back at Tubal: "You oaf, you country bumpkin, you do not understand the deeper mysteries. When you are in the House of Cain, you will do what I say!" Theron grabbed Zaava's arm and led her to his private chamber.

One hour later, Tubal and Aram were led to Cain's private dining room. Theron stood on one side and Zaava on the other side of Cain, who was sitting wearing a hooded shroud and eating a leg of lamb. Aram was amazed at how old Cain looked, and thought to himself: "How can this old man rule the City of Cain?" Then Cain stood up. Aram was shocked at how tall Cain was, even taller than Tubal. "Kneel, you infidels!" Theron barked. "Kneel in the presence of the most high priest!"

Aram quickly, and Tubal more slowly, dropped to their knees. Cain then commanded Zaava: "High Priestess Zaava, you have not been to the House of Cain in three years. Show your submission to me, show your husband who your master is." Cain glared at Tubal, challenging his authority. Then Cain sat back down and told Zaava: "Kiss the mark of Cain."

Without hesitation, Zaava moved in front of Cain, lowered her head, and kissed Cain on the forehead. Then she moved back to Cain's side.

Cain then addressed Tubal: "Zaava tells me that all is not well in the City of Gom. Can you not take care of a simple shepherd, Tubal?"

Tubal bitterly resented Cain's tone of voice. He shifted the conversation to business. "Enoch is inconsequential, Master Cain. He has not interrupted our business ventures."

"You misunderstand my concern, Tubal," Cain replied with firmness. "I am not concerned with Enoch's threat to our business enterprises. I am concerned about his threat to my authority."

"That's not my business," Tubal responded insolently.

"No, my arrogant Tubal, it is your business. I cannot have Enoch and that thug Arphaxad walking around preaching about their God. They are a threat to the cult of the Great Ebony Cow. They must be eliminated."

Aram was aghast. The mighty Cain, the most high priest, the man Aram had longed to meet, was talking about killing Aram's brother.

"Tubal," Cain continued, "I want Enoch and Arphaxad killed as soon as possible, and I want you to see to it."

Tubal stood firm. "No, Master Cain, murder is your business, not mine!"

Cain just chuckled. "Your insolence is at an all-time high, Tubal. If you were not such a good businessman, I would have you killed also."

"That would be your business, too," Tubal shot back.

Cain thought for a moment, then said: "I could offer you a fortune to kill Enoch and Arphaxad, but I won't. Zaava tells me that you and Enoch used to be childhood friends. Perhaps there is a sentimental streak under that hard exterior of yours, Tubal."

"I am a businessman, not an assassin."

"Well, I really didn't expect you to take the assignment, Tubal. I have already commanded Theron to head up the assassin squad." Tubal and

Aram turned to look at Theron, who smiled wickedly at them.

"Another thing, Tubal," Cain continued. "Zaava informs me that much preparation has been made for the building of the temple in the City of Gom. I am pleased with you and Zaava about that." Cain then turned his attention to Aram. "I understand that this young man desires to be a priest in the Temple of Gom."

Aram never felt smaller than when Cain gazed upon him. "I also understand that this young man is the younger brother of Enoch. Is that not correct, Aram?"

At the mention of his name, Aram stammered, "Y-Y-Yes, Most High Priest Cain."

"Excellent! Come here and kiss the mark of Cain."

Aram was weak-kneed at the prospect of kissing the forehead of the man who just ordered the murder of his brother. "Young man, you will never become a priest unless you kiss the mark of Cain."

Zaava spat at Aram: "Don't embarrass me now, Aram, after all I have done for you."

Aram, confused and undecided, looked over at Tubal. "Look, Aram, we cannot continue to be business associates unless you do as Cain says." Then, Zaava walked forward, took Aram's hand, and led him to Cain's chair.

"Kiss the mark of Cain!" Zaava demanded.

Aram, overcome and overwhelmed, leaned over and kissed the forehead of the Most High Priest Cain.

## Chapter Twenty-six

# Co-Conspirators

"Tubal, I want the Temple of Gom built within the next five years! Do you understand?" Cain bellowed.

"Yes, Master Cain, that kind of business I shall be happy to attend to." Then, Tubal turned to his wife and ordered: "Come, Zaava, let us return to our city."

"No!" Cain bellowed again. "Zaava shall stay with me to help Theron plan the attack on Enoch. That temple may never be dedicated to the Great Ebony Cow as long as the Sheep Man is alive. No, Tubal, you go on home and attend to your business, and your wife shall stay here to attend to mine."

Tubal muttered under his breath, grabbed Aram's arm, and muttered aloud as he turned to leave: "As you wish, Master Cain." Aram wanted to cry out that no harm should come to his brother, but the withering stare of Cain stifled any words from escaping Aram's mouth. Soon, Tubal and Aram were heading south, back toward the City of Gom.

Cain turned his attention to Theron and Zaava. "Theron, what are your plans for ridding the Earth of that pestilent Sheep Man?"

"The Sheep Man should be no problem, Cain. I'll take a few armed priests and go out and kill Enoch right away."

Zaava just laughed. Cain then asked her: "What say ye, Zaava?"

"Theron is a simpleton. It would take half a dozen armed priests just to overcome Arphaxad. My brother is as tall as you, Cain, and even stronger."

"Theron," Cain asked, "what do you say about that?"

"Well," Theron mused, "I guess Arphaxad would not stand idly by while armed priests killed Enoch. Perhaps, I should take a dozen armed priests with me."

"Zaava," Cain then asked, "will that be sufficient?"

"Really, Cain," Zaava replied, "Arphaxad is not my chief worry. Enoch is the dangerous one."

Theron questioned Zaava's sanity: "What could be so dangerous about the Sheep Man?"

"Enoch has a magic staff that performs miraculous feats," Zaava explained to the two men.

"I don't believe in miracles, Zaava," Theron laughed.

Cain looked cautiously at the young high priestess. "What so-called miraculous feats can Enoch do with his magic staff?"

"I saw Enoch wave that staff, causing two of Arphaxad's thug friends to freeze in mid-stride."

"Utter nonsense!" an incredulous Theron blurted out.

"How did Enoch do that, Zaava?" quizzed Cain.

"I don't know, Cain. But even worse, the Sheep Man waved that magic staff again, and a mighty roar and bolt of light shot out from the staff, striking Arphaxad in the neck, knocking him down, and almost killing him."

"This is preposterous, Cain," Theron challenged. "We should not listen to such obvious fabrications."

"Zaava," Cain asked, "did you see all of this with your own eyes?"

"Yes, Master Cain. I know all of this is hard to believe, and if I were Theron, I wouldn't believe it either, except I have seen it with my own eyes."

"Where does the Sheep Man get this so-called miraculous power?" Cain calmly asked.

"The Sheep Man, curse his demented mind, claims that the magic staff is a branch off of the Tree of Life in the Garden of Eden," Zaava answered.

"Ho! Ho!" bellowed Theron with great amusement. "This Sheep Man is a real religious fanatic! The Garden of Eden, my foot! Does Enoch really expect people to believe in fairy tales?"

"Arphaxad now believes in that fairy tale!" Zaava replied.

"Zaava, are you going to be the next one to believe in such fairy tales?" Theron sneered. Before Zaava could answer, Theron turned toward Cain and suggested: "Cain, if Enoch has any magic powers, he must get them from the same source that you get your power from -- from Satan. I think Enoch just wants to move in on some of your territory. But a small squad of armed priestly assassins and I can handle a couple of thugs like Enoch and Arphaxad."

Cain was thoughtful for a moment, then asked Zaava: "What do you think Enoch's intentions are?"

"Cain, though Theron is definitely older than I am and perhaps wiser, I think that he may not understand the Sheep Man as well as I do. Nonetheless, Enoch is certainly a threat to your cult of the Great Ebony Cow."

"Enoch shall most definitely die," Cain intoned. "How do you propose to do it, Zaava?"

"Cain, we cannot use just brute force against Enoch and Arphaxad. We must use stealth. We must overpower him before he can use that magic staff."

"Very well!" Cain concluded. "Theron, you and Zaava complete your plans this evening. I do not want to see either of you again until you bring me the magic staff of Enoch."

## Chapter Twenty-seven

# Surprise Attack

The next morning, Theron personally led a squad of twenty priestly assassins on horseback through the south gate. Hours before, two priestly scouts had departed to locate the whereabouts of the two traveling evangelists.

Meanwhile, Enoch and Arphaxad innocently continued their journey north toward the City of Cain. At each city along the way, Arphaxad and Enoch followed the same routine that they followed when they preached at the City of Gom. Arphaxad spoke first, speaking of the redeeming love and forgiveness of God, using as a human example how Enoch had forgiven him for kidnapping his daughter and selling her into slavery. Arphaxad always asked the city dwellers to personally forgive him for his awful deeds done in that city. Then, Arphaxad would introduce Enoch, the man who had walked with God.

Enoch then preached a powerful message of God's amazing grace toward a fallen race by promising to send a Redeemer Who would pay the penalty, the awful price for all of our sins. Enoch always warned the city dwellers that God's judgment would fall upon them one day if they did not repent of their sins and turn to God. At each city, Enoch urgently pleaded the city dwellers to believe in the coming Redeemer today.

In more than one city, several people responded to Enoch's urgent invitation. Lives were being changed through Enoch's faithfulness in obeying God's call upon him to preach.

The traveling evangelists kept walking northward at a slow pace. Although Arphaxad seemed to grow stronger by the mile, Enoch's limp, caused by that crushing blow to Enoch's leg so many months ago, seemed to become more exaggerated with each passing mile. Nonetheless, the two men were able to average about twenty miles per day toward their destination of the City of Cain.

One evening, having walked all day and meeting many passersby on the road north to the City of Cain, Enoch and Arphaxad stopped at a grove of tamarisk trees located next to a gentle stream running through a peaceful valley. "This reminds me of home, Arphaxad."

"Indeed, it does, my brother," Arphaxad replied. "It certainly seems like a nice, secure spot to me." The two men picked some fruit from nearby trees and made camp for the night. They sat, prayed, and ate, chatting about their many adventures during their preaching journey to the City of Cain. Arphaxad even admitted that the slow pace was good for him. "Maybe I am learning how to wait on the Lord, Enoch."

"But we have not yet faced much tribulation, my friend," Enoch cautioned.

"Don't pray for it, Enoch," Arphaxad jokingly warned. "I much prefer learning how to wait on God the way we have been learning it so far."

Both men praised God for how He had so far smiled upon their initial evangelistic journey. Soon, both men were tired and fell into a much deserved sleep. As always, Enoch slept with the staff of God at his side.

In the middle of the night, Enoch awoke from a nightmare. He had dreamed of being thrown into a deep pit, without food or water, As he awoke, he had a strange thirst in his mouth. He bounded up quickly and walked rapidly to the stream some twenty yards away.

As Enoch knelt down to cup some water into his mouth, he was startled by a scream: "Enoch!" Enoch jumped up and saw several men beating on Arphaxad with clubs. Enoch ran back to help his friend, but by the time he arrived, Arphaxad was knocked unconscious. Twenty-one men stood armed around the camp. The leader of the men, dressed in priestly array, stood in the midst of the camp, holding aloft the staff of God.

"Looking for something, my dear Enoch?" Theron said mockingly.

Enoch was brazen. "If you have hurt Arphaxad, I'll, I'll —"

"You will do nothing, you powerless prophet." Theron snapped his fingers and six priests moved forward and grabbed Enoch.

"Who are you?" Enoch demanded.

"Still cocky, I see," Theron replied. "Not that it will do you any good, but I am Theron, chief priest under the Most High Priest Cain, and these are my loyal assassin priests with me."

"What do you want from us? We have no silver. We have no gold."

"I don't want your silver or gold, Enoch," Theron said with a sickening smile. "I want your life."

"What have I done to harm you?" Enoch insisted.

"Dear Enoch, you underestimate yourself. Surely you know that you are a threat to the authority of the High Priest Cain and the cult of the Great Ebony Cow."

"No, Theron, God is a threat to Cain and his wicked cult," Enoch spat back.

"Ah," Theron sighed, "so you do speak of God. Personally, I think you are nothing but a common thug, just like Arphaxad, using religion to steal from people, just like Cain does. But you will never move in on Cain's territory."

"What are you going to do with us?" Enoch asked defiantly.

"Zaava and I have given that much thought, Sheep Man."

"Zaava!?! I should have known that she was behind this."

"Yes, Zaava is truly a wonderful person, don't you think, Sheep Man?" Theron chuckled.

"So Zaava wants me dead. What about her brother Arphaxad?"

"Him, too."

"She's a monster!"

"But what a delightful one, wouldn't you say, Enoch?"

"Go ahead, kill me," Enoch defiantly proclaimed. "Death does not frighten me. You cannot scare me, Theron, with the promise of seeing my Lord in Heaven this day."

"Ah!" Theron chuckled again. "Just as Zaava predicted. She said that you would not fear death, so she and I rejected a quick death for you. Zaava thought that she would get more pleasure from knowing that you died very slowly and very painfully."

Theron was delighted when he saw a flicker of fear in Enoch's eyes. "Ha! Your fear of death is as with other men, Sheep Man. Yes, we shall dig a pit, a very deep pit, and then throw you and Arphaxad in it. We shall next cover the pit with a large rock, with only a little opening for air."

Theron relished the plan which he and Zaava had so devilishly devised. "You and Arphaxad will first become thirsty, then hungry.

Within a few days, after much agony, you shall die."

Enoch glared at Theron, but drew strength from the God Whom he walked with. "My God is able to deliver us from the pit, and He will deliver us out of thine hand, Theron."

"You are a fool, Sheep Man, and soon you shall be a dead fool."

The following morning, at the break of dawn, Theron and his men led Enoch and carried the still unconscious Arphaxad to the middle of a dense, nearby forest, to a spot just a few feet away from a huge boulder. Then the twenty priestly assassins started to dig a pit, shallow at first, but then going deeper and deeper and deeper. With shovels and buckets and ropes, the priests were able to dig a pit thirty feet deep, but only four feet in diameter. "This is your grave, Sheep Man," Theron crowed, "your final resting place."

"No grave shall have victory over me, Theron," Enoch bravely responded.

"We shall see, Sheep Man, we shall see." Theron snapped his fingers and four priestly assassins knocked Enoch over, grabbed each limb, and held Enoch at the edge of the pit. Theron snapped his fingers again, and the priestly assassins tossed Enoch into the pit. Enoch bounced several times on the way down, then hit bottom.

Enoch never lost consciousness as immense pain filled his body. He was not sure, but the pain in his right leg was overwhelming, indicating a possible fracture. Just then, the sky above darkened. As Enoch looked up, he saw the still unconscious body of Arphaxad hurtling toward him. Enoch tried to move out of the way, but there was no place to hide. Arphaxad's limp, seemingly lifeless body landed with a sharp crack on Enoch's already painful leg. Enoch cried out as the waves of pain rolled over his body.

Then, the sky darkened again. With horror on his face, Enoch looked up at the boulder being moved in place over the opening of the pit. A small opening, no more than six inches wide, was left for air. As Enoch looked up, the evil, triumphal face of Theron appeared at the opening. "Look on my face, Sheep Man. It is the last face you shall ever see."

Enoch groaned within himself. With an amazing effort, he was able to say: "If you are so certain, Theron, toss down my staff."

Theron directed that the staff be brought to him. While Enoch waited, hoping against hope and praying like never before, he heard a sharp crack on the surface above. Theron then peered into the pit again. "Here's half a stick for a half-wit," he joked. Then Theron tossed the upper half of the staff of God down into the pit. "Farewell, Sheep Man, to you and your God."

Enoch could hear feet moving away from the pit. Then he heard horses' hooves in the distance, riding away from the pit. Enoch, between waves of agonizing pain, pondered his situation.

His right leg was broken. Arphaxad was unconscious, perhaps mortally wounded, and they were together trapped in the bottom of a thirty-foot, escape-proof pit. Before he passed out from the pain, Enoch uttered a final prayer: "Only You, Lord, can deliver us from the pit."

## Chapter Twenty-eight

# The Staff of Hope

Some time later in the afternoon, a bruised and battered and beaten Arphaxad slowly regained consciousness. His head was pounding inside as if his brain was trying to escape his skull. Through the pain he looked around at his surroundings. A faint light was glowing above him, far above him, at the top of a shaft of some sort. When Arphaxad looked up, he could see what appeared to be blue sky through a tiny opening in the shaft.

Arphaxad was able to make out the features of Enoch lying at the bottom of the shaft with him. Enoch, too, was bruised and battered. Even worse, Enoch's right leg was straight where the thigh bone is, but not straight at the lower part of the leg. "Where am I?" Arphaxad's mind recoiled. Arphaxad shook his traveling companion roughly, shouting, "Where are we?"

Enoch, in a fitful sleep punctuated by waves of pain, was startled into awakeness by Arphaxad's jostling, then moved to agony by the sound of Arphaxad's voice. "Aagghh!"

"Enoch! Enoch! Where are we!?!" Arphaxad yelled again.

Enoch groaned again, then put his right index finger up to his mouth to encourage Arphaxad to speak less loudly. As Enoch moved his right arm, his right leg moved slightly, causing another wave of excruciating pain to course through his battered body. "Aagghh!"

"Where are we?" Arphaxad whispered desperately.

Enoch could not respond through the pain. He tried to reach down to his right leg, causing even more pain to envelop his body. "Aagghh!"

Finally, Arphaxad asked another question: "What's wrong with your leg?"

Enoch answered through the pain: "It's broken."

"Yeah, I can tell, but where are we?"

Enoch looked up at his terrified companion, finally realizing that Arphaxad was in some sort of mortal terror of their situation. Gritting his teeth, Enoch replied: "In a pit."

Arphaxad's mind recoiled at the words. "Oh, no! Oh, no! OH, NO!"

Arphaxad's yelling made both men feel worse. "Calm down, Arphaxad!" Enoch whispered.

"How do we get out? How do we get out?" Arphaxad continued to rave.

"We can't, Arphaxad. We are trapped in here."

Arphaxad took one more look around his cramped quarters and cried out: "We're going to die!"

Enoch could not stand his friend's raving anymore. Aware of what agony he would cause to his body, Enoch reached over and slapped Arphaxad in the face.

Enoch's abrupt and violent action shocked Arphaxad out of his hysterical raving. The ex-thug started to whimper, "I'm sorry, Enoch. I guess ranting and raving won't help us much down here."

"No, I guess not, my friend."

"Enoch?" Arphaxad meekly pleaded.

"Yes," Enoch answered, still in agonizing pain from slapping his friend.

"Enoch, I have claustrophobia."

"What's that?" Enoch quizzed.

"Fear of small, enclosed places."

Enoch giggled, then chuckled. "My friend, you have a problem."

Arphaxad erupted again. "I have a problem? I have a problem? What about you, Enoch?"

"I don't have a problem," Enoch serenely replied.

"Aagghh!" escaped from Arphaxad's throat. "Here you are in a deep pit with no way out. Your leg is broken. And the other person in the pit with you is having a claustrophobic attack on top of a terrific headache. And you sit there saying you don't have a problem? You are weird, Enoch, really weird!"

Enoch just smiled, then said with some earnestness in his voice. "Arphaxad, I don't have a problem. God has a problem."

"Well," replied Arphaxad, "God's problem is my problem, and I want God to get us out of this awful pit."

"He will, my friend, He will."

"How?"

"I don't know that yet."

"When will you know?"

"I don't know that, either."

"I want to know, and I want to know now."

"We have to wait, Arphaxad, we have to wait on the Lord."

Arphaxad's shoulders slumped as he grew silent for a moment. The only thought in his head, in his pounding head, was the phrase Enoch had mentioned several times before: "Tribulation worketh patience."

Enoch then noticed that Arphaxad's head was severely bruised by the many blows to the head by the armed priests' clubs. Arphaxad noticed Enoch examining his forehead, and he reached up and touched his own head. "Aagghh!" the ex-thug cried out, recoiling from the pain. Through tears of agony, Arphaxad was able to whisper: "God certainly works in mysterious ways, Enoch. Here I now am with a bruised and crushed head in a pit with a man whose head I crushed and bruised last year."

"Life is funny sometimes," Enoch chuckled.

"Yeah," Arphaxad sarcastically replied, "I may die laughing."

Soon dark came, creating absolutely inky darkness in the pit. Arphaxad was terrified of spending a long night in such quarters. Both men slept fitfully, and both woke up grouchy the next morning.

"We are still here," Arphaxad dryly observed.

"So I've noticed," Enoch grouchily replied.

"God hasn't gotten us out of here yet," Arphaxad accused.

"So what do you want me to do about it?" Enoch grouchily accused back.

"I don't know, Enoch, but we must do something."

"Look, Arphaxad, if I knew what to do, I would do it." Then, Enoch stopped himself. "Hey, look, my friend, we shouldn't be arguing this morning. I know both of us are bruised, battered, thirsty, and hungry. Why don't we just pray to God to help us through this day?"

Arphaxad looked around at the limited space, looked up at the light streaming through the air hole above, and was reminded that God had not forgotten them. "You're right, Enoch. I am acting like a baby."

"Why don't you pray, Arphaxad?"

"All right." Then Arphaxad closed his eyes, and although the throbbing continued in his brain, he started to pray. "Lord, save us. Here we are, really in the pit. I don't know what to do, Lord. I am absolutely helpless. Only You can deliver us from the pit. Lord, please, save us. Until the Redeemer comes, Amen."

Arphaxad opened his eyes, then joked: "Looks like we are still here."

"But God is still here with us, my friend," Enoch replied. Then Enoch picked up the broken staff of God as a reminder of God's continued presence. As he looked at it, he blinked in the not-bright light at the bottom of the pit. He looked again, then screamed: "It's longer, Arphaxad, it's longer!"

"What's longer?"

"The staff of God."

Arphaxad looked casually at the staff of God which had been snapped in two by Theron. "It looks shorter to me, Enoch."

Enoch ignored his friend's remark and carefully examined the staff. Sure enough, the jagged end of the staff, where it had been broken in two, had become smooth again, and seemed to be an inch or two longer. "Arphaxad, yesterday Theron snapped the staff of God in half and threw the top part down here."

"You mean Theron, Cain's chief priest, is behind all of this?"

"Yes, both Theron and your sister Zaava plotted to have us killed out here on the road. His armed priestly assassins were the ones who beat you up the other night and threw us in this pit."

"Every brother should have a sister like Zaava," Arphaxad joked again.

"But, Arphaxad," Enoch went on excitedly, "after you and I were tossed in here, I dared Theron to throw down the staff of God. He took the staff, snapped it in two, and threw the top half down here."

"Yeah, but the staff still looks shorter to me."

"Don't you see, Arphaxad, yesterday the end of the staff was jagged. This morning, the jagged end is smooth."

Arphaxad grabbed the staff. "Are you sure, my friend?"

"Of course, I'm sure!" Enoch exulted. "God's at work, Arphaxad, I know it!" The two men did not have any food or water, but now they had something even better. They now had hope.

## Chapter Twenty-nine

# The Staff of Healing

The exhilaration of hope faded as thirst, hunger, and pain increased. That second night in the pit was especially difficult for Enoch, who added worry to his list of woes. As Enoch began sinking in the depths of despair, all of a sudden he heard a voice, a familiar voice, the voice of the Lord: "I will make thee unto this people a fenced brasen wall: and they shall fight against thee, but they shall not prevail against thee: for I am with thee to save thee and to deliver thee. And I will deliver thee out of the hand of the wicked, and I will redeem thee out of the hand of the terrible."

Enoch could hear the Lord, but he could not see Him. Nevertheless, Enoch was reminded that the Lord could see the plight of the two traveling evangelists trapped at the bottom of an escape-proof pit. As soon as Enoch took his mind off of his circumstances and lifted his gaze upward toward the Lord, his spirits lifted. As Enoch started to praise God, he fell into a deep, much needed sleep.

Enoch awoke before Arphaxad in the morning. As Enoch looked around the pit, his eyes spotted something unusual about the staff of God.

"Arphaxad!" Enoch yelled, "wake up! Look at the staff of God!"

Arphaxad groggily opened his eyes, recognized that he was still in the pit, then grumpily replied: "Let me go back to sleep. I was dreaming about a beautiful garden with fruit trees growing alongside a cool, fresh stream."

Enoch shook his friend. "Arphaxad, don't go back to sleep. You must look at the staff of God."

Arphaxad did not want to, but he finally lifted one eyelid and glanced at the staff of God. Then both eyes went wide open as his jaw dropped. The staff of God was at least three inches longer, and even more amazingly, it had sprouted leaves.

"Praise God, Arphaxad! God hasn't forgotten us!"

Arphaxad was indeed impressed, but as his empty stomach grumbled, then Arphaxad grumbled, too: "But you can't eat leaves."

Enoch agreed, then said: "God gave us leaves this morning for some reason, my friend. Let's pray."

As the two men prayed silently, Enoch's mind scanned his memory for the last time he had seen leaves such as these. When the answer finally came, Enoch smacked his forehead and astonished the still quiet, prayerful Arphaxad: "Of course!"

"Of course, what?" Arphaxad looked up dubiously.

Enoch was as gleeful as Arphaxad eating biscuits. "Arphaxad, these leaves are like the leaves on the Tree of Life."

"You mean the Tree of Life that grows in the Garden of Eden?"

"Yes! Yes! Of course! God broke a branch off of the Tree of Life to make this staff!"

"Well, that's wonderful, Enoch, but I am dying of thirst and hunger, and my head is banging inside like a gong. How are those leaves going to help us now?"

Enoch thought a minute back to the first time he had ever held one of the leaves from the Tree of Life in his hands, which had been scorched and blistered from crawling on the burning sand in the wilderness leading up to the Garden of Eden. "Could it be?"

"Could it be what?" Arphaxad asked in frustration.

"Hold still a second, my friend." Then Enoch gently pulled one of the leaves off of the staff of God, and tenderly moved the leaf toward Arphaxad's badly bruised and battered forehead.

"Hey, be careful with that, Enoch!" Arphaxad cried out.

"Just don't move at all as I gently rub the leaf on your forehead."

"Hey, that's going to hurt!"

"Don't be a baby, Arphaxad. Now just don't move." As Enoch began to rub the leaf on Arphaxad's forehead, two amazing things happened. First, the bruises disappeared immediately. Then, as Arphaxad touched his smooth-as-baby-skin forehead, he cried out: "All of the pain is gone! Hallelujah!" Arphaxad jumped up, almost knocking over Enoch, and he started dancing around the pit, accidentally bumping Enoch's broken leg.

"Aarrgghh!" Enoch cried out as an amazing burst of pain enveloped his entire body. Arphaxad looked down at his friend, stopped dancing, and apologized profusely. "Oh, I'm so sorry, Enoch. I'm really sorry. Sometimes I get so carried away. Please forgive me. Does it hurt?"

The pain swelled up in Enoch's leg. "Take a look at my leg, Arphaxad," Enoch grimaced.

As Arphaxad knelt to examine the leg, he almost gagged. Infection had set in all around the fracture area. The leg was pus-filled and swollen to twice its normal size. Arphaxad was just glad that there was nothing in his stomach to vomit. As he turned his eyes away, Enoch asked: "How does it look, my friend?"

Arphaxad had no tact. "You are going to die, my friend, unless you get immediate treatment for that leg. It is badly infected and swollen."

Enoch's spirits sagged as the pain kept coursing through his body. Then Arphaxad, in a moment of inspiration, snatched another leaf off of the staff of God. As he moved the leaf toward Enoch's swollen right leg, Enoch cried out: "Hey, be careful with that, Arphaxad!"

Arphaxad ignored his friend's pleading. "Just don't move at all as I gently rub the leaf on your leg."

"Hey, that's going to hurt!"

Arphaxad chuckled. "Don't be a baby, Enoch. Now just don't move." As Arphaxad gently rubbed the leaf on Enoch's leg, the infection disappeared immediately. Right before their amazed eyes, Enoch and Arphaxad watched as the swelling in his leg shrunk and shrunk and shrunk until his right leg was normal size. "All of the pain is gone, Arphaxad! All of the pain is gone! Hallelujah!" Enoch jumped up, almost knocking over Arphaxad, and he started dancing around in the pit. "I'm healed, Arphaxad. God healed me!" Then both men, with little grace and style, started to jump up and dance around in their little confined space like two little kids.

## Chapter Thirty

# The Staff of Life

While Enoch and Arphaxad were learning lessons on patience the hard way, Theron and his cohorts returned triumphantly to the City of Cain. Theron rode straight to the priestess house to report his success to Zaava.

Theron was escorted to Zaava's private chamber, where her maid was brushing her long, beautiful hair. "I am most pleased to report to you, Lady Zaava, that we captured the Sheep Man so effortlessly, just like you plotted."

"Very good, Theron. Did you toss Enoch and Arphaxad into a deep pit?"

"Yes, Lady Zaava," Theron exulted.

"Are you sure that there is no way out of that pit?"

"There is no human way possible for those two thugs to get out of that pit. We dug it thirty feet deep and capped it with a huge boulder."

"How long can they last in there, Theron?" Zaava quizzed.

"Healthy men could only last three or four days without water, but neither of them were very healthy when we left them."

"Oh, Theron, I so much love death. The Sheep Man shall bother me no more." Zaava smacked her lips in delight. Then she added: "Before we report the death of Enoch to Cain, let me have Enoch's magic staff."

Theron proudly produced the lower half of the staff of God. "I broke that magic staff in two. It will do no more magic for the Sheep Man."

Zaava shrieked with terror: "What have you done, Theron? Where is the other half of the staff?"

Theron recoiled from Zaava's outburst, then nervously answered: "I tossed that useless broken staff down to that powerless Sheep Man."

"You idiot!" screamed Zaava. "You idiot!"

"What's wrong, Zaava? What did I do wrong?"

Zaava jumped up out of her chair, stomped around the room, and kept yelling: "My plan was perfect! My plan was perfect!" Then she stopped, looked directly into the terrorized eyes of Theron, and shrieked even louder: "Who knows what Enoch can do with even half a staff!?!" While Theron cowered under Zaava's withering stare, she demanded: "You must go back right now and make sure that the Sheep Man is dead!"

"But I can't, Zaava," Theron stammered. "Cain already knows that I am back. He is expecting an audience with you and me in just a few minutes."

"Just shut up, you fool!" Zaava retorted. "I can handle Cain. You take your men back immediately to where you left Enoch. Bring back the rest of the magic staff to Cain, and bring back Enoch's body to me."

"You seem to know the Sheep Man better than I, Lady Zaava." Theron admitted. "I shall do as you say."

"How soon will you be back with Enoch's body and magic staff?" Zaava demanded.

"They are about two days' hard ride south of here. My squad and I should be back in four or five days."

"Excellent! Report to me immediately upon your return."

Theron turned and walked rapidly out of the priestess house. Even while his men were feeding and brushing down their tired horses, Theron announced that they would be leaving immediately on fresh mounts. The squad members grumbled, then quickly saddled new horses. None of them dared to disobey the command of Chief Priest Theron. Soon, Theron, mounted on a white steed, and the twenty priestly assassins charged out of the south gate of the City of Cain.

Meanwhile, a well-rested and well-healed Arphaxad started to complain again. "You know, Enoch," Arphaxad grumbled as his stomach grumbled again at the bottom of the thirty-foot tomb, "my forehead feels great, but my tongue is still dry and my belly is still hungry."

Enoch, whose tongue and stomach felt the same as Arphaxad's, nonetheless calmly and assuredly replied: "Fret not, Arphaxad. Our God shall supply all our need according to His riches in glory."

"I would gladly give all the riches of the world for one cup of cool, clear water right now," Arphaxad dreamed. Then the stark reality of their situation weighed heavily upon the ex-thug's heart -- no water for three days. They could not survive much longer. That evening the two men were very quiet, trying to save all of the moisture and all of the energy in their bodies. That night, Arphaxad dreamed the same dream again -- he was in a beautiful garden with fruit trees growing alongside a cool, fresh stream. Arphaxad could only smile in his sleep.

The next morning Arphaxad awoke first. His lips were parched and his tongue seemed to stick to the roof of his mouth. He momentarily thought that perhaps it would be best to just go back to sleep, forever.

But Arphaxad was concerned for his friend Enoch. He looked over at his friend, lying so still in a fetal position on the other wall of their escape-proof pit. "One day soon, maybe tomorrow, both of us will never awaken again."

As Arphaxad looked with affection on his doomed friend, his eyes glanced at the staff of God on the ground beside God's prophet. Arphaxad rubbed his eyes, and then looked more carefully at the staff. He could not believe his eyes. "Surely I am still dreaming," he told himself. He rubbed his eyes again, then pinched his wrist, then exclaimed softly to himself: "I'm not dreaming!"

"Enoch! Enoch! Wake up, Enoch!" Arphaxad breathlessly cried. Enoch, so absorbed in sleep, at first did not respond. Arphaxad nudged his friend and screamed: "Wake up! Wake up!"

Enoch slowly opened his eyes and could not imagine why the usually grumpy Arphaxad was so excited this morning. "Let me go back to sleep," Enoch sighed.

"Enoch, don't go back to sleep," Arphaxad pleaded. "Look at the staff of God, man. Look at the staff of God."

Enoch glanced at the staff lying on the ground beside him. Enoch's eyes nearly bugged out of their sockets -- several branches had sprouted from the staff of God, and on each branch grew fruit, all manner of fruit, springing forth from the staff of God.

Enoch jumped up, turned his gaze to Heaven, lifted holy hands, and started crying. "Oh, thank You, God. Oh, thank You, God." Then Enoch looked again at the staff of God, delighted with the problem of choosing which he would eat first -- an apple, an orange, a pear, or a banana. Arphaxad and he started laughing almost hysterically as each one of them grabbed an orange and started peeling. As they sunk their parched mouths into the life-giving fruit, they both knew that they had never before tasted anything so juicy and delicious.

The two men feasted for breakfast that morning and the next as God provided a new crop of fruit on the ever-lengthening staff of God. Enoch praised the Lord continually for the Almighty God providing all their needs. The two men were so grateful for God's bounty as God nourished them each day. But it was not too long before Arphaxad became anxious again. "Enoch, God is indeed supplying our every need, but . . ."

"But what, my friend?" Enoch questioned.

"But we are still in the pit."

## Chapter Thirty-one

# The Staff of Deliverance

On the fifth day after the entombment of Enoch and Arphaxad in the thirty-foot pit, Theron and his squad of priestly assassins returned to the dense forest area where they had labored so hard to wipe Enoch and Arphaxad off the face of the Earth. As they approached the spot where the huge boulder was that covered the pit, Theron could not believe his ears -- loud, joyful singing was emanating from the pit.

At about the same time, Enoch heard the sound of approaching hooves. "Arphaxad, listen! I hear horses and riders. We are saved, Arphaxad, we are saved!"

Arphaxad stopped singing and listened carefully to the sound of many hooves. "More than likely, my friend, our captors have returned to finish us off."

"You are always so negative, Arphaxad," Enoch wishfully responded.

Just then, the horses pulled up some distance away from the boulder. Footsteps, many footsteps approached. A face peered down from the air hole above. Arphaxad flippantly greeted the chief priest: "How's it going, Theron?"

Theron's jaw dropped several inches. "I can't believe it. I thought you were dead."

"Nope!" replied the ex-thug. "We are alive and well at the bottom of the pit."

Theron still could not believe it. "How have you two managed to stay alive?" Theron asked incredulously.

Arphaxad then tossed a large orange up toward the air hole. Theron instantly jerked his head back away from the projectile. "Where in the world did you two get fruit down there?"

"From the staff of God," Enoch answered. Then he playfully offered: "Why don't you come on down and join us?"

"Do not mock the chief priest of the cult of the Great Ebony Cow!" Theron stiffened. "Your God may have kept you alive this long, but your luck has now run out." Theron then raised up and barked an order to the priestly assassins. "Gather stones and pile them on the south side of the pit."

The tired assassins reluctantly obeyed. Soon, a large pile of stones lay next to the pit. Then Theron commanded the weary assassins to shove the large boulder away from the opening of the pit. As the exhausted assassins were struggling to move the boulder, Arphaxad suddenly turned serious. "What's your battle strategy now, Enoch?"

"I don't know, Arphaxad, but God will show us in due time."

"In due time? My soul, Enoch, we don't have due time. We are about to become human pancakes."

Slowly, the boulder was moving away from the opening to the pit. Arphaxad was becoming frantic. "Do something, Enoch, for God's sake!"

"Let's pray, Arphaxad," Enoch serenely replied. Enoch bowed his head, closed his eyes, and prayed silently to the Lord: "Dear Lord, we are still in the pit, about to be crushed by stones. We need You, Father. You are our only hope. Please save us!"

Then the word of the Lord came unto Enoch: "Smite the ground."

Arphaxad could not hear the word of the Lord. All he could see was that Enoch was slipping into some sort of a trance. The ex-thug shook his friend roughly: "Enoch, wake up. Do something!"

Enoch then looked up. As the boulder was finally moved away from the opening to the pit and the priestly assassins had picked up the stones to smash down upon the heads of the two helpless men below, Enoch softly said to Arphaxad: "Stand back."

Arphaxad stepped back, clinging to the side of the wall. Just as the priestly assassins raised the stones above their heads to fling down into the pit, Enoch smote the floor of the pit with the staff of God.

What happened next happened so quickly that no one had time to react. A mighty, rumbling sound filled the air as the ground underneath shook violently. The priestly assassins and Theron were frozen in terror as a mighty explosion blew Enoch and Arphaxad straight up into the air, catapulting the two trapped men out of the pit, through the air, and into the branches of a nearby tamarisk tree.

The earth then trembled again and the ground near the pit cracked wide open. Theron and his men stumbled and started to slide into the widening pit. The earth shook again and the pit started to cave in. As all the men slid wildly into the pit, the earth shook violently one last time. A mighty explosion blew the boulder straight up into the air as if it were a mere child's toy. Then, as Theron and his squad of twenty men slid all the way down to the bottom of the pit, the boulder came crashing straight down out of the sky. With a sickening thud, the boulder landed at the bottom of the pit, completely crushing Theron and the entire squad of priestly assassins. The earth stopped shaking, and no more sounds were heard from the bottom of the pit.

Long after the earth stopped quaking, Arphaxad's knees continued to quake up in the tamarisk tree. Enoch, marveling that he and Arphaxad were still alive, climbed down from the tree and told Arphaxad to join him. But Arphaxad held on to the branch for dear life. "Climb on down, Arphaxad," Enoch pleaded. "It's safe now."

Arphaxad whimpered up in the branches: "You don't understand, Enoch. I was raised in the city. I am afraid of climbing trees."

Enoch laughed at his friend's predicament. "God has delivered you from the pit. I guess I will have to deliver you from the tree." After a few hesitant attempts, Enoch was finally able to coax his friend out of the tree. They then walked cautiously toward the pit.

As Enoch peered into the pit, Enoch gratefully said: "The Lord has brought us up out of an horrible pit." Arphaxad turned his head away from the scene below. "You know, Enoch," Arphaxad said, shaking his head, "Theron dug the pit and is fallen into the pit which he had dug. His mischief returned upon his own head."

Enoch peered down into the pit one final time, then lifted his voice to Heaven: "I will praise the Lord according to His righteousness: and will sing praise to the name of the Lord Most High."

As the two survivors walked away from the pit, Arphaxad saw Theron's white steed and another of the horses of the priestly assassins. "Let's return those two horses to the City of Cain, Enoch," Arphaxad suggested.

"Let's ride," Enoch replied.

## Chapter Thirty-two

# City of Knowledge

When Theron and his squad of priestly assassins failed to return within five days, Zaava became extremely nervous. Her anxiety led her and her maid to camp out at the south gate of the City of Cain, so eager was she to see the dead body of the Sheep Man.

On the morning of the sixth day after Theron had left the city to finish off Enoch and Arphaxad, Zaava was frantic. "What's taking Theron so long?" she cried out to her ever-present maid. Just then, as a crowd of travelers was approaching the south gate, Zaava's maid pointed to a white horse in the distance: "My lady, isn't that white horse yonder Theron's steed?"

Zaava jerked her head in the direction of the white horse. She breathed a great sigh of relief as she recognized Theron's steed. Then her maid wondered: "But who is that riding on the steed, my lady? It does not look like Theron."

Zaava's heart stopped for a moment. As she strained to make out the distant horseman, her mind and schemes were perplexed. "Who could that be on Theron's horse?"

As the travelers neared the south gate, Zaava's maid cried out: "Why, my lady, that does appear to be your brother Arphaxad riding on Theron's steed, and that man Enoch on the horse at his side. That man Enoch appears to be holding a staff."

Zaava's jaw dropped to her chest and stayed there for several minutes. As the crowd of travelers passed through the south gate of the City of Cain, very few even noticed the well-dressed lady and her maid gawking at them. As Enoch and Arphaxad finally rode by, Enoch did not even look over in Zaava's direction, but Arphaxad waved and cheerfully greeted his gawking sister: "Good morning, dear sister. It is so good to see you again."

Zaava remained speechless and turned very pale. "My lady," the maid asked, "are you feeling all right?"

Zaava slowly regained her composure as the two riders slowly disappeared into the crowded marketplace. "I'm fine, I think. Let's go back to the priestess house. I must freshen up a bit before I report this unfortunate bit of news to Cain."

Meanwhile, Arphaxad was giving Enoch a guided tour of the City of Cain, the City of Knowledge. Enoch's mind recoiled at many of the same features of the city he had seen the last time he had ventured to Cesspool City -- the marketplace for slaughtered beef, lamb, pigs, and other animals, the marketplace for men and women offering their bodies to other men and women for a price, and the sickening slave market. Finally, Enoch asked his friend if they could visit one of the beautiful buildings which housed the various schools for which the City of Knowledge was renowned. "The School of Philosophy should intrigue you, Enoch. Obviously, when I lived here before, I did not spend much time there."

The School of Philosophy was a magnificent edifice several stories high, one of the most beautiful man-made structures which Enoch had ever seen. Arphaxad explained that each floor had its own different school of philosophy. As they approached the front door, which was two double doors sixteen feet high swinging out toward the marketplace, the doorkeeper to the building noticed the thug Arphaxad walking toward him. "I doubt that anything inside the School of Philosophy would interest you, Arphaxad," the doorkeeper chided. "The slave market is further down the street."

Enoch chuckled: "Your reputation precedes you, my friend."

"My friend and I would like to visit one of the classes."

The doorkeeper set his jaw firmly. "We don't let the likes of you in such a fine place as this, you thug."

Arphaxad was just as resolute as the doorkeeper. Stepping forward one more step and looking down at the doorkeeper, the ex-thug firmly asked: "Are you going to stop me?"

The doorkeeper looked up at the ferocious-looking thug and started to sweat: "Uh, sure, go ahead, Arphaxad."

As Arphaxad and Enoch swept by the nervous doorkeeper, the ex-thug looked over at Enoch and calmly said: "My reputation precedes me."

As the two men marveled at the ornate grand hall leading into the School of Philosophy, Arphaxad asked his friend: "Which school do you want to visit?"

Enoch was just awed by the intricate latticework walls, columns, and ceilings in the grand hall. "I did not know that man was capable of such accomplishments, Arphaxad."

"Yes," the ex-thug replied, "the same city that produces such magnificence also produces the slave market outside. Now, which school of philosophy would you like to visit?"

Enoch's mind was still enthralled by the monumental architecture of the grand hall. "Uh, I'll let you choose, Arphaxad."

"OK. Let's go up to the top floor and visit the school that your friend Tubal would occasionally visit when he was in the City of Cain."

Enoch's attention immediately diverted to Arphaxad upon mention of his old friend Tubal. "Which school is that, Arphaxad?"

"The School of Humanism. We will have to walk that sparkling spiral staircase all the way to the top floor."

"Lead the way, my friend," Enoch eagerly replied, enraptured by the beauty and grandeur of the staircase leading to the top floor. As the two travelers reached the second floor, Enoch enthused: "This spiral staircase upward is a marvel of invention and beauty."

"Yes, my friend," a less admiring Arphaxad replied, "but the spiral also leads downward." As the two men reached the top floor, they stepped just inside a classroom where a teacher was lecturing his students. "Man is the measure of all things. Our great City of Cain has led the world in cultural development because we humanists have freed man from the bonds of religious tyranny. Without the restraints of religion, man is able to imagine, to explore, to create. We humanists have encouraged man to develop himself to his fullest capacity. The technological progress of our age is made possible only through the unshackled creativity of the mind of man."

Enoch leaned over to Arphaxad. "Why, this man seems to elevate mankind to god status." Arphaxad quieted his friend as the lecturer continued.

"We must do our own thing. When you open your mind to all of the possibilities in the world, then you shall become as gods. Unshackle yourself from all forms of authority, including religion and your own parents. Then, and only then, you shall become your own god."

Enoch stepped outside of the classroom, followed by Arphaxad. God's prophet whispered to his friend: "That guy has got to be kidding."

"No, Enoch," the ex-thug replied, "that hogwash is standard teaching in the School of Humanism."

"Does anyone take that stuff seriously?" Enoch asked in wonder.

"Many parents pay through the nose to send their children to hear that twaddle."

"That lecturer can't be very bright, Arphaxad."

"To the contrary, Enoch. That lecturer is one of the smartest, most powerful men in the City of Cain."

"What's his name?"

"Lamech-Cain."

"Is he related to Cain?"

"Sure. Most of the people around here are descendants of Cain one way or another. I wouldn't mess with Lamech-Cain. He is one of the most vicious men in the city."

Enoch scratched his head for a moment, then asked his friend if they could visit another class. Arphaxad asked: "Any particular school?"

"Are there any that teach about God?"

"Surprisingly, yes," Arphaxad replied. "If we walk down that spiral staircase to the first floor, we can observe a class on Basic Philosophy and Religion."

"Let's check it out." As they walked down the ornate staircase, Enoch was not nearly as enthralled with its beauty.

When they reached the first floor, they stood in the back of another classroom, where another lecturer was talking to a younger group of students. "We have been examining the various gods of the Earth. People of the Earth variously worship the sun, the moon, trees, frogs, and so forth." The lecturer displayed various idols which mankind had carved with its own hands. "Of course, the official religion in our wonderful city is the worship of the Great Ebony Cow." He then pointed to a two-foot high statue of a black cow.

The lecturer continued. "Our religion is probably the most highly developed of all religions. Many of the earlier religions sacrificed lambs and other animals. Indeed, our own cow religion retains vestiges of cow worship. However, under the able direction of our great High Priest Cain, we have advanced to more effective and religious sacrifices -- human sacrifice."

Enoch, the prophet of God, could hold his tongue no longer. "Doesn't anybody in this city worship the God of Heaven?" he spoke out in the classroom.

The professor was very smooth. Noticing Enoch's obviously country and uncouth attire, he knowingly replied: "Ah, you must be one of the country folk who worship that most ancient and outdated religion begun by Cain's father. I do not know of anyone in the City of Knowledge who still believes in such primitive religion. We city people have advanced far beyond such a nebulous concept of an unknowable God in some nebulous faraway place called Heaven. Rather, we now have gods made of gold, of silver, of stone, of wood, all graven by man's own artful and imaginative devices."

The lecturer could tell that Enoch was not impressed by his comments. The lecturer next said: "But, of course, dear country fellow, we people of the City of Cain would never seek to deprive you of your right to worship any god you wanted." The lecturer motioned to Enoch and Arphaxad to follow him to a plaque several feet below the statue of the Great Ebony Cow. "Come here. Read this."

Enoch and Arphaxad hesitantly walked forward to the plaque. The professor brightly commented: "We want you and everyone else to feel at home here in the City of Knowledge. If we do not have an idol of your own god, then maybe this plaque will satisfy you."

Enoch read the plaque: TO THE UNKNOWN GOD.

## Chapter Thirty-three

# The Tower

Cain slapped Zaava across the face. "I should have you killed for permitting Enoch and Arphaxad to arrive in my city." Then Cain slapped her again. "Now tell me, what has happened to Theron and his squad of priestly assassins?"

Zaava meekly cried: "I don't know, Master Cain."

Cain struck her again. "Zaava, you have disappointed your master. I gave you a simple task -- to kill the Sheep Man and that thug brother of yours, and you blew it." Cain turned his back on Zaava. "I wonder," he said softly after regaining control of his emotions, "if I can trust you to handle the task of high priestess of the City of Gom."

Zaava cried out in agony as her future plans were threatened. "Master Cain, I can handle Gom myself. It is Theron's fault that the Sheep Man and my brother are not dead."

Cain just shrugged. "You can't get good help anymore. Theron is probably dead, Tubal is too independent, and Zaava is too incompetent."

"Master Cain, let me prove my competency to you. Let me go back to the City of Gom and build that temple to the Great Ebony Cow."

Cain paused for a moment, lost in thought. Then he turned back toward Zaava and shouted: "Get back to the City of Gom where you belong." Zaava breathed a great sigh of relief. "But what shall happen to my brother and the Sheep Man?"

Cain sneered: "I will handle them myself." After booting Zaava out of his room, Cain called another priest to send spies throughout the city to locate the prophet of God and his companion.

Meanwhile, Enoch and Arphaxad departed the School of Philosophy and calmly walked down the main street of the city. As they stopped at a fountain for a drink of water, Arphaxad expressed his worry: "Cain will stop at nothing to see us dead, Enoch."

"I know that, Arphaxad. We are marked men. But I am not going to let the threat of death deter us from testifying and preaching in this wicked city."

"So what's your plan, Enoch?" Arphaxad queried.

"I don't know yet."

"Well, don't take all day."

"I know what I want to say, my friend, but I just don't know when and where."

"Why not here and now?"

"Be patient, Arphaxad. Perhaps you have a plan."

"I was kind of thinking we could preach in some inconspicuous place, get done in a hurry, then leave this town quickly. I don't like it here."

"That is a bold plan," Enoch chuckled sarcastically.

"So you want to be bold, huh, my friend?" Arphaxad said defensively. "Well, if you want to be bold, why don't you preach from atop the Tower?" As soon as he said those words, Arphaxad had a feeling that he shouldn't have.

"That's it, Arphaxad!"

"That's what?"

"We shall speak from the Tower!"

"I was just kidding, Enoch."

"I'm not. The Tower is an excellent place for everyone in the city to see and hear us."

"That's dumb, Enoch. That's really dumb. Maybe we can get up to the top of the Tower, but how will we get down?"

"God will find a way."

"But remember," Arphaxad started to whimper, "I don't like heights."

"I never knew that. I thought you were just afraid of climbing trees."

"Ever since I found my father hanging from the rafters, I have been afraid to climb to any great height."

Enoch looked upon his friend with compassion. "We will have to overcome that fear through the power of God, Arphaxad. But I am confident that you hit upon the right idea of preaching from atop the Tower." The two men walked along the main street to the very center of the city. Arphaxad almost fainted as he looked up to the top of the Tower, where rested the wicked Temple of Cain.

The Tower and Temple of Cain was the largest man-made object on Earth, rising two hundred feet from the ground, the symbol of the power as well as the depravity of Cain and his city. The Tower literally towered over everything, as Cain imagined his own personality and life force towered over everything on the face of the Earth.

Arphaxad turned toward his friend. "I don't think we can climb this thing, Enoch."

"What's wrong, Arphaxad? Are you afraid? The Lord will be with us."

"Enoch, I had forgotten about the ten-foot high fence surrounding the base of the Tower and the pit at the east end." As they walked up to the fence, Enoch was impressed by the quality of the wrought iron fence which encircled the Tower. As Enoch fingered the fence, he asked: "Is this the fence which was built in your father's blacksmith shop after your father died?"

"Yeah," Arphaxad replied, "I hate this fence and I hate this Tower."

"How do we get on the other side of the fence?" Enoch queried.

"I really don't think we should do this," Arphaxad pleaded.

Enoch ignored Arphaxad's fears and worries. "Isn't there a gate somewhere?"

"The only gate is on the north side."

"Then let's walk around to it." As they walked around the eastern side of the fence, Arphaxad continued to protest. "I don't think we can get in, Enoch. Look up ahead. There is an armed priest guarding the gate."

Enoch looked up ahead, where he could see a priest standing with a spear right in front of a large, intricately designed gate on the north side of the fence. As they walked closer, Enoch asked his friend: "Do you recognize the guard?"

"Oh, no!" Arphaxad exclaimed. "It looks like Maxmil."

"So you two have met before?"

"I killed his brother several years ago. He hates my guts."

"Good. You can apologize to him after we ask him to let us through the gate."

"Enoch, you have got to be kidding. Maxmil will never let us enter the gate."

"Don't worry, Arphaxad. I've got an idea."

"It better be a good one. Maxmil has spotted us." Just then the armed guard raised his spear and shouted at the two approaching men. "Why, Arphaxad, you dirty, rotten, murderous thug! Don't come any closer or I will put this spear right through you."

"Uhh, good morning, Maxmil," Arphaxad stuttered as the two men ground to a sudden halt. "Hey, listen. I really am sorry about your brother. I want to make it up to you somehow. Can you forgive me?"

Maxmil was not in a forgiving mood. "You are sorry, all right, you imbecile. Don't you know that Cain has his spies out looking for you?" Just then, Maxmil motioned to a spot behind the two men. "Look!" he shouted.

Just as Arphaxad and Enoch turned their heads to see if any spies or other armed priests were approaching from behind them, Maxmil leaped forward and thrust his spear at Arphaxad's chest. But Arphaxad, who never did quite learn to trust the motives and intents of armed priestly guards, pivoted out of the way as quickly as a cat, grabbed the advancing spear, and threw Maxmil to the ground. Before Maxmil knew what was happening, he was lying flat on his back with Arphaxad holding his spear to his throat.

"Don't kill him, Arphaxad!" Enoch screamed.

The ex-thug relaxed his grip on the spear as Maxmil looked up in terror. "Go ahead and kill me, you thug. If you don't, Cain will."

"Maxmil," Enoch pleaded, "we really wish you no harm. All we want to do is enter through that gate." Enoch bent down and pulled the key ring off of Maxmil's belt. Enoch then walked over to the gate, inserted the key, and opened the very heavy gate. While Maxmil looked on with evident terror at the open gate and the spear at his neck, Enoch walked back over to him.

"Maxmil, I am going to try to save your life. In just a minute, Arphaxad and I are going to walk through the gate. Then I will shut the gate door and throw you the key. Then, I want you to lock the gate behind us, run to Cain's house, and bring other guards. You will probably get a reward for capturing us."

Now, it was Arphaxad's turn to look at Enoch in terror. "Are you crazy or something, Enoch?"

Enoch ignored his friend. "Do you agree, Maxmil?" Enoch asked.

Maxmil delighted in seeing Arphaxad's terror. Realizing that his options were very limited, Maxmil declared: "It's a deal."

Enoch then dropped the key next to Maxmil's head and said: "Back off of him, Arphaxad. Let's go through the gate." The ex-thug hesitated to give up his prey and to walk into a trap. "Now!" Enoch exclaimed.

Arphaxad then removed the spear point from Maxmil's throat, and walking backward with the spear still aimed in the direction of the now-unarmed guard, entered through the gate with the prophet of God. Maxmil leaped to his feet, breathed a quick sigh of relief that he was still alive, then quickly snatched his key and shut and locked the gate behind the two men, trapping them inside the grounds of the Tower of Cain. "Fools! You fools!" Maxmil exulted in victory.

Before Maxmil sped off to announce his capture of the two men, Enoch called to him one more time. "Maxmil, there is one more thing I have for you." The guard examined Enoch warily, then asked: "What do you have that I want?"

"We need to return your spear," Enoch calmly replied. Arphaxad jerked his head toward his friend and asked incredulously: "You want to do what, Enoch?"

"Toss the man his spear, Arphaxad."

"Ah, Enoch, let me keep it. It gives me a warm sense of security."

"God is our fortress and defense, Arphaxad. Toss the spear over the fence and let's start climbing."

Arphaxad scratched his head, then turned toward Maxmil. The ex-thug let out a grunt, causing the guard on the other side of the fence to stumble backward and fall. Arphaxad let out a laugh, then gently tossed the spear over the fence. "Hey, Maxmil, I really am sorry about your brother. Would you please forgive me?"

The rearmed guard could only shake his head after getting up from the ground and grabbing his spear. "You guys are crazy!" Then Maxmil turned and ran toward Cain's house.

Enoch was already standing on the first of hundreds of steps leading up the spiral path to the top of the Tower. Arphaxad was hesitant to follow. "Come on, Arphaxad. Just one step at a time."

The ex-thug almost fainted again as he craned his neck to look how high up the Tower was. Then he cautiously walked forward and started climbing the steps behind Enoch. Higher and higher the two men climbed the spiraling staircase, finally coming into view of the marketplace, where thousands of shoppers were jammed into the sprawling street. One of the shoppers spied the two men on the staircase. "Look! At the Tower! Two men are climbing the Tower!"

A few, then more, then hundreds, then thousands of eyes turned to look at the two men slowly climbing the winding staircase up toward the Temple of Cain atop the Tower. Soon, all activity in the marketplace ceased as even the hundreds of vendors watched with amazement as two unlikely looking fellows were climbing up to the sacred temple.

About halfway up, Arphaxad stopped, took a breath, and made the mistake of looking down. He almost fainted again. "I can't go on, Enoch. I can't go on!" he cried.

Enoch didn't even look back at his terrified friend. "Just keep looking up, my friend. Just keep looking up!"

## Chapter Thirty-four

# Preaching from on High

"People of Cain," Arphaxad bellowed across the marketplace from atop the Tower on the east platform, "you all know me -- Arphaxad the thug!" Every ear in the marketplace below strained to hear the words of the familiar figure atop Cain's sacred Tower. "I come to you today with a message that can change your life as it has changed my life. I come to you today with a message of love and forgiveness."

Thousands of people in the marketplace below whispered to the persons beside them: "What's that he is saying? I must not be hearing him right." They quieted down as the thug -- the ex-thug -- continued his message.

"I have offended many of you, I have stolen from you, I have killed your friends and loved ones, and I have kidnapped your children. I am sorry, truly sorry, for all of those offenses against both God and man."

The multitude below again whispered: "What's that? The thug mentions some sort of a god!"

"Today, people of Cain, I come to you grieving over my offenses. I seek your forgiveness. Please, in the name of God, forgive this former thug."

The crowd stirred. The words and tone of the voice of Arphaxad were entirely unexpected, even startling. "Former thug!?!" many of them thought. The masses below listened intently as Arphaxad continued to preach.

"One man has already forgiven me. Just a few months ago, I had bashed this man's head in with a shittim club, and then I kidnapped his young daughter and sold her into slavery." Tears started to well up in the ex-thug's eyes as he continued to testify. "Yet, that same man, whom I offended so deeply, has found such great love in his heart to forgive me."

The crowd again stirred. "What kind of man could forgive a thug like Arphaxad?" many of the city dwellers below asked to themselves.

Arphaxad continued to testify. "That man, that bruised and battered man, was able to forgive me for all of the sins I had committed against him because that man's sins had already been forgiven by God. Dear friend, when your sins are forgiven you by God Himself, then and only then can you find true love, true joy, and true peace in this world. I want you to now listen to the man who helped me -- Arphaxad the thug -- to find love, joy, and peace in this world. Please, please, I beg of you, please listen to that man -- Enoch, the prophet of God."

Arphaxad stepped back and Enoch stepped forward. The prophet of God had never before spoken to such a monstrous crowd, numbering in the tens of thousands. God's prophet was more than a little intimidated, especially when he spied a phalanx of priestly guards advancing toward the Tower from the north, led by an old but obviously vigorous man in a hooded robe. Enoch's mouth went suddenly dry and his knees started knocking. "Lord," he cried, "give me Your strength and Your words."

Then, as Cain's contingent approached the gate to the Tower and tens of thousands of ears were waiting for Enoch to speak, the prophet finally opened his mouth. "People of the City of Cain, as I passed through your magnificent School of Philosophy today, I found a plaque with this inscription: TO THE UNKNOWN GOD. This day, Him declare I unto you."

The multitude below marveled that still another man would dare to speak of God from the top of the Tower of Cain, where Cain's temple was the source of worship of another god. Enoch, with the first few words out of his mouth, became emboldened to preach. "God that made the world and all things therein, seeing that He is Lord of heaven and earth, dwelleth not in temples made with hands; neither is He worshipped with men's hands, as though He needeth any thing, seeing He giveth to all life, and breath, and all things."

Cain reached the gate below and ordered Maxmil to open the gate. Cain was enraged by Enoch's speech. "One Lord of Heaven and Earth indeed!" Cain muttered to himself as Maxmil fumbled with the key and lock. "This Sheep Man is seditious and dangerous!" he yelled at Maxmil. "Why did you let him inside the gate, you idiot?"

Just then, Maxmil unlocked the gate and flung open the heavy iron entrance to the Tower. "They are trapped inside, Master Cain!" Maxmil pleaded. Cain yelled again, "You stupid fool!", then grabbed Maxmil's spear and thrust it through Maxmil's stomach. As Maxmil fell backwards, holding the spear, fatally wounded, Cain barked to the other armed guards: "If those two men up above escape from my hand this day, the same thing that happened to Maxmil shall happen to each of you." Having gained the full attention of his guards, Cain issued his final order: "Thrust those two men through with your spears, but save their bodies for me. I, Cain, the Most High Priest, shall alone have the honor of throwing those two men off of the Tower." As the guards started up the steps to the temple and platform above, Cain followed them at a slower pace, eager to hear every word dripping from the seditious Sheep Man's lips.

"God hath made of one blood all nations of men for to dwell on all the face of the earth, that they should seek the Lord, if haply they might feel after Him, and find Him, though He be not far from every one of us."

Cain cursed Enoch while the founder of the city and its absolute ruler continued to slowly climb the steps. "The guards will pierce you through in just a minute, Sheep Man. There is no escape from the Tower of Cain."

Enoch, meanwhile, observed the guards climbing the steps, with the old man trailing behind. But God gave His prophet boldness. "For in God we live, and move, and have our being."

The crowd in the huge marketplace was visibly moved by the drama set before their very eyes and ears. For hundreds of years, the city dwellers had been ruled by the murderous tyrant Cain, who made every city dweller recite the slogan: "For in Cain we live, and move, and have our being." Enoch's words, certainly seditious and incredibly revolutionary, brought new life and hope to a people long chained in bondage to Cain's treacherous and evil cult of the Great Ebony Cow.

Just then, the armed priestly guards reached the top of the Tower, near the temple. On the other side of the top of the Tower was the east platform extending out over the flaming pit below, which had not been ignited for this special, unexpected worship service. Before Enoch could say another word, the whole marketplace could hear the words of Cain as he was still climbing the steps: "Kill them! Kill them!"

The guards instantly obeyed and dashed across the floor of the temple towards the two men who were standing on the east platform. As the guards raised their spears to throw at Enoch and Arphaxad, the prophet of God raised his staff over his head and waved it in the sky. Instantly, a bolt of light shot across the top of the Tower, just above the heads of the onrushing guards. A loud rumble, louder than anything the guards or anyone else in the City of Knowledge had ever heard, roared across the marketplace. The guards were stunned, shocked into immobility, their spears still held aloft, ready, willing, but unable to obey the command of Master Cain.

The bright light in the sky and the loud rumble so startled Cain as he was climbing that he had to grab the iron railing to avoid falling backward down the steps. He alone of the thousands of people in the marketplace and on the Tower was unable to see what had happened above. As he gathered himself and resumed climbing, Cain was utterly amazed at the sound of the next voice that he heard. Enraged, Cain started running up the steps to the top.

"God now commandeth all men everywhere to repent: Because He hath appointed a day, in the which He will judge the world in righteousness by that man whom He hath ordained, the coming Redeemer."

Just as Enoch spoke the words "the coming Redeemer," an old man in a hooded robe reached the top of the Tower. Enoch turned to Arphaxad and asked his friend: "Who is that?"

"Cain."

Enoch stared into the eyes of High Priest Cain from the other side of the platform. The high priest was doubled over, hands on his knees, breathing very heavily from his mad dash to the top of the Tower, speechless, red-faced, unable to move. Enoch felt no fear from the pitiful old man on the other side of the temple. The prophet of God turned his gaze from Cain back toward the multitude in the marketplace below. "Repent! Repent! Seek the Lord! He is not very far from every one of us. For in God we live, and move, and have our being."

Enoch paused as he took one final glance at the throng of people in the marketplace below. Then, he turned toward Arphaxad and motioned that it was time to depart. As the two men swirled and headed back toward the steps, Arphaxad passed the guard closest to him and tweaked his cheek. As the two men of God passed the heaving Cain, who was still gulping for air, Enoch paused and looked closely into the wild eyes of Cain, full of fury, yet impotent. Then the two men started down the steps, Arphaxad graciously permitting Enoch to lead. When they reached the bottom, Enoch saw for the first time the lifeless body of Maxmil just outside the gate. Tears formed in the prophet's eyes.

The two men walked through the gate and headed toward the city's south gate. The vast multitude divided as the prophet and ex-thug passed through the marketplace, through the south gate of the city, and into the countryside beyond. It was a great and glorious day, long remembered and long retold -- a prophet of God had preached the Words of God in the City of Cain.

# Part Three

# Spreading the Good News

## Chapter Thirty-five

# Jared and Meshach

"Well, preacher, what do we do now?" asked Arphaxad as the two evangelists walked south.

"I believe we have finished our first journey for God," Enoch beamed with satisfaction. "Let's head back home!" After walking for several hours, the two walkers, physically exhausted from their stunning triumph at the City of Cain, found a nice secluded spot to camp for the night. Within minutes, safe within the everlasting arms of the Redeemer, both men were fast asleep.

The next day, and for many days thereafter, they journeyed south. Enoch, who started to feel a strong need to visit his father, suggested that Arphaxad and he stop by Jared's homestead. Enoch's mind was especially centered upon his younger brother Aram, who, when Enoch visited home last, was still a happy, young shepherd. But now, Enoch cried to himself, his brother was caught in the same net of materialism that ensnared Tubal.

The two travelers arrived at Jared's homestead around lunchtime, when everyone was inside getting ready to eat. When Enoch knocked, his mother Rachel answered the door. She just stood there, stunned, surprised to see her oldest son. Then she gave him a quick hug and told Enoch to stay put at the door. Enoch thought the greeting strange, but he waited obediently.

After a slight commotion inside, Enoch could hear someone else walking to the door. As the door swung open again, Enoch's unsmiling father glared first at Arphaxad, then stiffly said to his son: "I am surprised to see you, my son. Aram warned us that you might run into trouble in the City of Cain."

"Have you seen Aram recently, Dad?" Enoch achingly quizzed.

"A couple of weeks ago, son. He filled us in on your recent activities. Enoch, I am ashamed of you."

"What!?!" Enoch asked incredulously. "Ashamed of what, Dad?"

"Aram said that you have become a religious fanatic, trying to force your new-found religion down people's throats. I won't have any of that here, son."

Enoch was shocked as Jared continued. "And Aram said that you have been trying to ruin his new career with Tubal. Now, Enoch, family members have to help one another, not hurt one another."

"Dad, I can explain. And there's so much more I want to share with you."

"You can come in, my son, if you promise to behave," Jared said as if speaking to a naughty child. "But you have to leave that thug outside."

Enoch was flabbergasted by his father's rudeness and inhospitality. "Dad, Arphaxad is my friend."

"Friend!?!" Jared screamed. "You call the man who kidnapped my granddaughter your friend? What kind of monster have you become, Enoch?"

"But Dad, God has forgiven him and so have I."

"Well, my God hasn't forgiven him and neither have I. Leave him out here, Enoch. No thug will enter my home."

Enoch started to shake. "Arphaxad is with me, Dad," he firmly stated.

Arphaxad, who had become increasingly uncomfortable as this conversation continued, finally interrupted. "Ahhh, go ahead, Enoch. I'll be all right out here. Go in and be with your family."

Enoch stood firm. "Arphaxad and I are family -- brothers in the Lord. Where I go, he goes," Enoch spoke prophetically.

"He's not welcome here, son!" Jared replied just as firmly, as he slammed the front door in the faces of the two forlorn men. Enoch just stared at the door for a minute, unbelieving at first, then shocked, then crushed. When no one returned to the front door, Enoch finally hung his head in shame and started to walk away, followed by Arphaxad, who was grieving for his friend.

The two men walked in silence for miles

-- one unable to speak, the other afraid to speak. Finally, after building up enough courage, Arphaxad weakly said: "I'm sorry, Enoch. I really am sorry."

Enoch struggled for words as tears streamed down his face. "It's not your fault, my brother," Enoch sobbed as his knees collapsed under him. For many minutes, the prophet of God lay on the ground, pounding it with his fists, crying out: "Why, God? Why?"

After a crying spell, Enoch rose from the ground, shook off the dust, and resolutely declared to his friend: "Let's go see Sarah's folks."

"Is her father as friendly as yours, Enoch?" Arphaxad hesitantly replied.

Enoch almost let out a chuckle. "No, my brother, Sarah's father Meshach is a believer. He encouraged me to seek God last year."

"Then what are you waiting for, Enoch?" Arphaxad yelled as he started heading down the road. About dinnertime, after walking westward all afternoon, Enoch spotted the familiar homestead of Meshach the farmer.

Arphaxad was greatly relieved that Meshach and Opal and all of the kids still at home were excited to see the ex-thug as well as Sarah's husband. Arphaxad had never seen such a large, warm family before. He revelled in their goodness and kindness toward him as well as their evident love for the Lord, just like at Enoch's homestead, with the notable exception of

Methuselah. While Arphaxad was stuffing his hungry face at the eating table, Enoch started telling Meshach and the others about how Enoch had gone searching for Adam and how he had found Adam, or rather Adam and Obstinate the Goat found him. Meshach was thrilled that Enoch had mentioned Meshach's name to his dear, old ancestors, Adam and Eve.

Little Miriam became scared and started to cry as Enoch described the wilderness and his encounter with the Devil. Enoch called to the little girl and had her sit in his lap as he continued his story: "But the Devil didn't get me, Miriam!" Miriam was greatly relieved.

Everyone was fascinated as Enoch told about the two cherubim, the Garden of Eden, and then the Lord Himself. Never before had that dear family of believers heard such an amazing story of God's grace, deliverance, and salvation.

Then, Enoch described his return to his homestead and his eventual showdown with the thug Arphaxad at the City of Gom. Miriam turned toward the one and only Arphaxad, who had a biscuit stuffed in his mouth. "You were a mean, mean man!" the little girl accused. Arphaxad just raised his eyebrows, swallowed the rest of the biscuit whole, and then gulped. "Let Enoch finish his story, little Miriam," Arphaxad pleaded.

Everyone cheered as Enoch told the exciting story of the bolt of light flashing from the staff of God and striking the thug and knocking him off of the platform. Arphaxad just kind of hunkered down lower in his chair at that point. Then, as Enoch explained how God saved that wicked thug, Arphaxad sat up straight and smiled broadly. Everyone cheered again and came over and gave the ex-thug warm hugs. Arphaxad, overcome with emotion, started to cry. His mind raced back to his first encounter with Enoch. He vainly tried to say: "I'm sorry about little Crista. Would you all please forgive me?"

Everyone quickly forgave the ex-thug, who was welcomed into Meshach's family as Uncle Arphaxad. Then Miriam said: "Uncle Arphaxad, be quiet now as Enoch tells the rest of his story." Arphaxad just smiled crookedly at the little girl as Enoch finished his story. All of the children were cheering as Enoch described the miraculous escape from Theron's pit; then they laughed as Enoch pictured the big, tough Uncle Arphaxad cowering in the tree limbs. Uncle Arphaxad just shrugged.

Meshach was especially intrigued by the confrontation on top of the Tower of Cain. "You have struck a blow for freedom, my son," Meshach exulted cautiously. "But you can be sure that Cain will strike back."

"He's a mean, mean man," little Miriam added, looking up at Enoch.

"Fear not, little one," Enoch replied comfortingly. "Greater is He that is with us than he that is in the world."

## Chapter Thirty-six

# Methuselah and Martha

Enoch and Arphaxad finally made the long journey home. As they reached the top of the hill overlooking Enoch's homestead, Arphaxad stopped a minute, took in the scene of the house wherein he was saved not too long ago, and gently sighed: "It's so good being home."

As the two road-weary travelers started walking down the dogwood-lined path to the house, Sarah, Methuselah, and Elihu all spotted them and started running up the path to meet them. The two boys were eager to hear of the adventures of the traveling evangelists. As everyone settled inside in the common room, and after the two men gulped down several glasses of orange juice, Elihu asked again: "Tell us what happened on your first journey."

Even Methuselah was impressed as Enoch and Arphaxad told the stories of their exciting escapes from the clutches of Theron and Cain. For a minute, Methuselah even entertained the thought that perhaps the prophet business was not so bad after all. "But I love being a shepherd," he reminded himself.

Sarah and the boys begged the two men to stay home for awhile, which is just what they did. For several months Enoch and Arphaxad stayed home to help plow up the garden, to help tend the sheep, and to even build an addition to the house for the expanded number of people living there.

Too soon for Sarah, Enoch and Arphaxad announced that they were going on another missionary journey, this time south. The next day the two evangelists headed to parts unknown, where thousands of people in numerous cities heard, for perhaps the first time, the good news of God's love, redemption, and salvation. As in cities north of the City of Gom, many people eagerly responded to the invitation to accept the gift of eternal life.

Soon, a pattern developed in Enoch's household. The two men would return home for awhile to help with the harvest and to plant a new crop. Then, they would head out to preach in new cities and to follow up on converts in places where they had already seen fruit. One of the least fruitful of the cities wherein they preached was the City of Gom. Enoch's good friend Ludim comforted Enoch with the observation that a prophet is without honor in his own country.

One of the few converts in the City of Gom was little Martha, who was growing into a lovely young lady with an even more lovely spirit. As Methuselah grew older, he sought more and more excuses to visit the City of Gom so he could drop by to visit Ludim, Perna, and incidentally, the lovely young Martha.

Elihu, on the other hand, did not pay much attention to girls. From time to time, he did ask Enoch or Sarah about Crista. Her parents started to wonder if Elihu carried a secret love for Crista in his heart. Perhaps he, too, was eager for God to fulfill His promise to return Crista to her family.

Aram continued to live with Tubal and Zaava, much to Enoch's distress. He, too, seemed uninterested in marriage, but Ludim explained why to his friend Enoch. "Your brother doesn't want anything to hold him back in his business dealings. Besides, I hear he is a heavy contributor to Zaava's temple, which is now in the early planning stages." Enoch was shocked that Tubal and Aram were actively engaged in planning and procuring building materials for a proposed temple right in the center of the city.

Lalomar continued to be Zaava's lackey, even giving up his precious candlestick business to devote himself full-time to Zaava's enterprise of building the Temple of Gom. Enoch was shocked at the evil influence of the high priestess of the City of Gom.

Ludim then shared the most dreadful news of all. "Zaava now has recruited her first priestess to assist her in her evil desires."

"Anyone I know?" Enoch innocently asked.

Ludim lowered his eyes, softly shook his head, and answered: "Elam's daughter Adah."

"Adah?" Enoch screamed. "Crista's old playmate? How can that be, Ludim?"

"When Adah turned eighteen, she fulfilled a lifelong dream and ran away from home. She always did love the city. She hated the country desperately, even more so after Elam was saved. She never wanted anything to do with her father's new-found religion."

"Elam must be crushed, Ludim."

"Yes, my friend, Elam and his wife Bildah have taken it very hard. Elam, of course, blames himself for how Adah has turned out. He often says he wishes that you had talked to him earlier about the Redeemer."

Enoch paused for a moment, thinking back to how he had misled his family for so many years in empty, formalistic ritual, and how his own son Methuselah seemed to lack any desire to have a close, personal relationship with God. "Elam must have hope, Ludim. God can change the heart of the worst sinner. We must have hope." Enoch later attempted to visit with Adah and to tell her about the Redeemer's great love for her. But Adah was not interested in the least, so smitten was she by the sights and sounds of the city. Her goal in life was to help Zaava and Tubal build the greatest temple in the world outside of the temple in the City of Cain.

As the years floated by, as Enoch and Arphaxad continued their missionary journeys, Methuselah and Elihu developed into responsible young men, perhaps earlier than most boys in their late teen years. One day, while Enoch and Methuselah were alone tending the sheep many miles away from the homestead, the son asked the father if they could have a man-to-man talk. Enoch looked into his son's eyes and realized, perhaps for the first time, that his son had matured into a man. Methuselah came right to the point: "Dad, I want to marry Martha."

Enoch was silent for a moment as he continued searching his son's eyes. The father saw an evident sincerity behind the still youthful features of his son. Then Enoch said: "You certainly have fine taste in women, son. Martha is a very fine young lady."

Methuselah kept talking: "Do I have your permission to ask Ludim for her hand in marriage?"

"Have you prayed about this, son?"

"Dad, I don't pray as much as you do, but yes, I asked God to please let me marry Martha."

Enoch suppressed a grin. "Did God approve of your idea?"

"Dad, are you making fun of me? This is serious."

"Yes, it is serious, son. This is no laughing matter. I deeply appreciate your coming to me to discuss this matter of the heart."

"Well, then, do I have your permission to talk to Ludim?"

Enoch grimaced, unsure of how to respond. Then, he slowly and solemnly replied: "You certainly have my permission, son. But I don't want you surprised and I don't want you crushed if Ludim initially turns you down."

Enoch's words hit Methuselah like a dart. "Why would Ludim turn me down?" he shot back.

"Methuselah, are you a believer?"

"Well, no, Dad, not in the way you believe. I'm not sure if I can trust in God the way you do."

"It's not complicated, son," Enoch commented. "Anyway, Martha is a believer, isn't she?"

"Yes, Dad, and she is also a wonderful person who also happens to love me."

"You don't understand, Methuselah. Ludim will not permit Martha to marry an unbeliever. God strictly forbids it."

Methuselah seemed prepared for that answer. His response stung his father. "Wasn't Mom a believer when she married you?"

Enoch gasped for breath. "You've really been thinking about this, haven't you, son?"

Methuselah pressed to improve his advantage. "Well, it's true, isn't it? You were not a believer when you married Mom. So why can't I marry Martha?"

"Son," Enoch replied as he tried to gain control of himself, "it is true that I was not a believer back then. But I thought I was a believer, your mother thought I was a believer, and I even had Meshach believing I was a believer. But it is different with you and Martha, son. You know, and Martha knows, and Ludim knows that you are not a believer."

Methuselah grew tired of wrestling with his father's old-fashioned concepts. "Martha and I love each other and I want to marry her."

Enoch tried to be tender. "Son, I think that Martha would make a wonderful wife for you. I am very fond of her. But, if she truly loves you, then she won't marry you."

"We will just see about that!" shouted Methuselah as he made up his mind to visit the City of Gom as soon as possible to ask Ludim for the hand of Martha in marriage. The following week, after returning home from grazing the sheep in the hills with his father, Methuselah made his long-awaited trip into the city. Just as his father had prophesied, Methuselah was surprised and crushed when his beloved Martha told him that she could not marry him.

"But, Martha, I thought you loved me!" the young man cried.

"I do love you, Methuselah. I will wait for you, my love." And wait she did, for one hundred and fifty years.

## Chapter Thirty-seven

# Zaava and Adah

## 720 A.C.

Over the years, while Zaava and Tubal were busily engaged in making preparations for the construction of the Temple of Gom, Elam's daughter developed into a fruitful priestess for Zaava, indeed too fruitful. One morning, young Adah left her bedroom, walked down the hall, and knocked on Zaava's door.

"Come in," an imperious voice sounded from within.

Adah slowly opened the door and peeked inside. Zaava was still in bed, even though it was late morning. "What do you want, Adah?" Zaava snapped.

"May I talk with you for a moment?"

"Just for a moment," Zaava again snapped. "I am a very busy woman."

Adah looked sheepishly at the woman lounging on her bed. "Zaava, I uh, I uh . . ."

"Out with it, woman!" Zaava said with disdain.

"Zaava, I uh, have a problem."

"Don't we all, dearie," Zaava replied as she examined her fingernails.

Adah, by now accustomed to Zaava's uncaring attitude, was nonetheless hurt this morning. "Oh, Zaava, help me! I am in trouble!"

"What kind of trouble, dearie?" said Zaava airily.

Adah again looked sheepishly. "Zaava, I uh, I uh . . ."

Zaava grew impatient with poor Adah. "Out with it, you little twerp!"

Adah could hardly speak as she started to shake. Finally, she managed to blurt out: "I am expecting a child."

The words struck Zaava with great force. Zaava tumbled out of bed, strode over to the quivering Adah, and slapped her across the face. "You stupid idiot!" she screamed. "You stupid idiot!" she repeated as she slapped the defenseless, expectant mother again.

Adah just stood there and cried. Zaava finally recovered herself and bluntly told the pregnant woman: "Well, you will just have to do what I always do when I get in that situation."

Adah was confused. She had never known that Zaava was ever in that delicate condition. Adah meekly asked: "What do you do, Zaava?"

Zaava looked straight into Adah's eyes: "You will have to get an abortion."

Adah was still confused and did not respond immediately. With an innocency born of the country, she asked Zaava: "What is an abortion?"

Zaava just laughed. "You can take the girl out of the country, but you can't take the country out of the girl." Then she laughed some more. "The more cultured and sophisticated of us ladies of the City of Cain have been practicing abortion for years."

"But what is it?" Adah asked again, ever hopeful of becoming as cultured and sophisticated as Zaava.

Zaava smiled fiendishly: "Very simple, dearie. You shall kill your baby while it is still in the womb."

Zaava's words struck Adah like a sledge-hammer, numbing her mind as it recoiled from the awful shock of Zaava's words. Adah shrunk back from the still smiling Zaava. Finally, little Adah blurted out: "Kill my baby!?! Never!"

Zaava was sickened by the tenderheartedness of her priestess apprentice. "You little slut. How do you ever expect to become a great high priestess like me if you continue with such provincial attitudes?"

"I will not kill my baby!" Adah insisted hysterically as she ran out of Zaava's room and back to her own.

Zaava was startled by Adah's intransigence. "Cain was right. You can't get good help anymore." Then the high priestess went over to her vanity and rang for her maid. As her maid spent countless minutes stroking Zaava's long, black hair, Zaava sat and thought about what to do with her wayward priestess.

Meanwhile, young Adah, heartbroken, stunned, confused, locked herself in her room all day. All of her dreams, all of her hopes, seemed dashed by the expected birth of her child. Yet, in her heart, she knew that she could not be as Zaava suggested -- a murderer of her own child. Adah wept herself to sleep that night, haunted by terrible nightmares.

The next morning, Zaava herself brought up some breakfast for her wayward charge. She slowly approached Adah's door and knocked gently.

"Who is it?" Adah cried.

"It's me," Zaava replied softly.

"Get away from me, you murderer!" Adah screamed.

Zaava was prepared to knock down Adah's emotional defenses. "Oh, I am sorry, Adah. I did not mean to be so cruel to you yesterday. How thoughtless it was of me, especially in light of your delicate condition."

Adah was momentarily confused by Zaava's momentary sweetness. "What do you want?"

"Dear Adah, I have spent a long night thinking about your baby. I certainly want you to have your baby. I won't let anyone suggest that you abort your darling child."

Adah was not yet mollified. "Do you

promise, Zaava?" she demanded.

"Of course, dear," Zaava quickly responded. "Would I ever lie to you?"

"I want my baby!" Adah insisted.

"Of course, dearest Adah," Zaava continued. "Your baby shall be born. Please let me bring some breakfast to you. You and your baby must be starving."

Adah was not sure what to do. Should she trust Zaava? If not, whom could she trust? She knew that she could never go home again. She was confident that her father and mother were too ashamed of her to ever let her in the house again. Perhaps Zaava did have a change of heart. Finally, after a battle in her heart, young Adah timidly walked over to the door. "Do you promise that my baby will be born?"

"Oh, yes, dearest Adah."

Adah unbolted her door and let Zaava in.

Zaava was holding a tray with a large breakfast of eggs, ham, and biscuits. Adah's mouth watered when she saw all of the delights. "Go lie down, dear Adah," Zaava ordered sweetly and with much concern. "You must take care of yourself and your little baby." Adah eagerly complied. As she ate the large breakfast, Zaava shared her plans with the poor pregnant girl. "Adah, Tubal tells me that we have all the building materials we need to start building the temple."

"Oh, that's wonderful," Adah brightly replied in between mouthfuls of ham.

"Adah, we are now ready to start building the temple. I have ordered Tubal to have the temple ready for its dedication ceremony in about six months. And Adah . . ." Zaava said expectantly.

"Yes, Zaava?"

"I have decided that we should not dedicate the temple until after your baby is born."

"Oh, Zaava, that is very thoughtful of you. I would surely hate to miss the dedication of the grand Temple of Gom."

"In fact, Adah, I want you and your precious little baby to be guests of honor at the dedication ceremony."

Adah squealed. "Oh, Zaava, I have been so wrong about you. Yesterday, I thought you were the most wicked, evil person on the face of the Earth. But today, Zaava, today you have proven me wrong. Would you please forgive me, dearest Zaava?"

"Oh, I do, dearest Adah, I do," Zaava said with great earnestness as she moved forward and gave Adah a hug. "Just trust me, Adah. I will take good care of you and your baby." Adah beamed as Zaava patted Adah's belly. Adah dreamed of one day holding her baby in her own arms. Zaava dreamed of the day, six months or so in the future, when the Temple of Gom would be dedicated to Cain by the sacrifice of the first-born of Zaava's priestess.

## Chapter Thirty-eight

# The City of Shorr

That same day Enoch was hoeing the weeds in Sarah's herb garden. Suddenly, he heard a familiar voice: "Enoch! Enoch!" Enoch dropped his hoe and looked up in the sky. "Yes, Lord? Here am I."

"You and Arphaxad have been faithful to preach of Me. You must go and preach again."

Enoch dropped to his knees. "Oh, Lord, I am truly an unholy and unworthy servant. I need Your grace, Your power, Lord, and so does my family."

The Lord was pleased with his prophet's petition. "Your petition shall be granted, Enoch. Now, travel southwest, preaching along the way, until you come to the City of Shorr on the shore of the Great Sea. There I shall be glorified."

Enoch was so humbled to have the God of the universe speak thus to him. "Thy will be done, Lord."

"And one final thing, Enoch," the Lord concluded.

"Yes, Lord?"

"Be back home in exactly six months, six months to the day."

"Thy will be done."

When Enoch made his announcement at lunch of the Lord's visitation in the garden, everyone, including Methuselah, was eager to hear of the Lord's command. "The Lord wants Arphaxad and me to travel all the way to the Great Sea."

Sarah, Elihu, and Methuselah beamed while a frown crossed Arphaxad's face, unnoticed by the excited prophet. "Hey, Dad, I would love to go sailing on the Great Sea!" blurted Methuselah.

"Well, son, I don't know if Arphaxad and I will go sailing or not. All I know is that God wants us to preach there."

Sarah looked wistfully. "Dear, do you think that you and I could some day travel to the Great Sea together?"

Enoch looked carefully at his wife's face as she spoke those words. "Sarah, would you like to go on this trip?"

"Oh, no, dear. It's just that some time I would like to be with you as you travel."

Enoch could see the yearning in Sarah's heart. "Dear, one day, Lord willing, you and I, just the two of us, will take a nice, long, leisurely trip together."

"Do you really mean that, Enoch?" Sarah pleaded.

Enoch got up from his chair and walked over to his wife, gave her a kiss on the cheek, and softly said: "Let's start praying about it tonight."

All of a sudden, Sarah did not mind so much that her husband was taking off on another evangelistic journey.

The next morning Enoch and Arphaxad were on the road again. After traveling and preaching for several months, they neared the City of Shorr. "Have you ever seen the Great Sea, Arphaxad?" Enoch asked.

"Sure, my friend. Arphaxad has seen everything. Have you ever seen it, Enoch?"

"No, I sure haven't, Arphaxad. Until I started searching for God and then traveling for Him, I had never done much traveling. Is the Great Sea big, Arphaxad?"

"Bigger than you can ever imagine," Arphaxad replied. "Our God made a very big world." Enoch was becoming more and more curious to see the Great Sea with each approaching step.

That evening, just before sunset, the two traveling evangelists reached the top of another hill. There, in front of them, spread out from horizon to horizon, was the Great Sea. Enoch hardly noticed the beautiful City of Shorr below him as his gaze was transfixed by the glorious beauty of the setting sun, casting reflections of the brightly colored sky off of the brilliant blue waters of the Great Sea. Enoch had never before dreamed of such beauty on God's green and blue Earth. His heart suddenly yearned to be with Sarah, who more than Enoch would glory in the beauty of the setting sun.

"Kind of impressive, isn't it?" Arphaxad muttered.

Enoch just stared for several minutes as the reds and yellows and oranges changed color before his very eyes. Seeing all of the different colors caused a light to go on in Enoch's mind. "Hey, Arphaxad, how far does the ocean go?"

"There are many lands beyond the oceans, Enoch, very far away," the ex-thug replied as authoritatively as he could.

Enoch looked misty-eyed toward the far horizon. "The people in those faraway lands need to hear the Words of God."

Arphaxad was jolted by Enoch's simple observation. "Wait a minute, brother!"

Enoch did not bother to even look at his friend. "Why, don't you agree that there are great multitudes beyond who need to hear the good news of the coming Redeemer?"

Arphaxad had a look of terror upon his face. "Maybe they do, but this landlubber isn't going to tell them. I get seasick every time I take a boat ride."

Enoch turned and smiled at his closest friend. "Arphaxad, you are a constant source of surprises. When are you ever going to learn? If God wants us traveling overseas to preach, then we will go."

"If God wants me to go, I will go, but not in one of those ships anchored below at the City of Shorr," Arphaxad said defiantly.

Enoch peered down at the several ships anchored in the beautiful harbor below. "How else would you get overseas then?"

"Remember those two cherubim in the Garden of Eden?" the brave ex-thug answered his friend.

"Of course I remember the cherubim. What do they have to do with crossing the ocean?"

Arphaxad was bold as well as imaginative. "The way I see it, the only way you will ever get me overseas is to fly me across the ocean."

Enoch roared with laughter. "Why don't you pray about that, my imaginative friend?"

"Listen, Enoch, you pray that God sends us across the ocean and I will pray that He doesn't." With that concluding remark, Arphaxad led the way down the road to the City of Shorr.

## Chapter Thirty-nine

# Preaching Aboard Ship

The City of Shorr was a typical seaport of that day. The main street leading into town went by many brightly colored homes, through the vast marketplace where exotic goods and foods from all over the world were bought and sold, and finally down to the docks, the economic heartbeat of the city. Enoch loved the smell of the sea as he and Arphaxad walked closer and closer to the docks.

A dozen or so ships were either docked at the piers or were sailing into the harbor. Enoch was certain that his son Methuselah would love to go sailing one day on one of the ships. Enoch himself looked forward to traveling overseas to preach the gospel in faraway lands and also to look for his long-missing daughter.

The sailors milling around the docks came in so many different colors that Enoch was simply flabbergasted. "Arphaxad, where do all of these sailors come from?"

Arphaxad just smiled and waved at several groups of sailors on the docks. "These sailors are from places all over the world. Be careful with them, though, Enoch. They can be a pretty rough bunch."

"Do you know any of them, Arphaxad?"

"Yeah, sure, Enoch. I have visited Shorr several times."

"Arphaxad, if we preach the gospel here, and some of these sailors become believers, then they can take the good news of the coming Redeemer back with them to their homelands."

"That sounds like a better idea to me than our traveling on those ships to those homelands. But I don't know how much success we will have with sailors. Their language and habits are not exactly heavenly." As they continued to walk in the area of the docks, Enoch heard some coarse language such as he had never heard before. Plus, there were several other evidences of the soaking corruption of the dock area that seemed to permeate the air, like the smell of seawater.

The two men stopped near a ship where a crowd of people was gathered. Sailors and other folks in the City of Shorr were listening intently as some strangely garbed character from some faraway country was making a speech from the forward deck of the ship moored at the pier. Enoch and Arphaxad could hear the man talking about "the innate goodness of man," and that "God, if there really was a God, was a God of love Who would never send anyone to Hell." The two evangelists were intrigued by the message as the speaker flamboyantly described the God that he did not even know for sure existed. When the speaker finally paused for a moment to catch his breath, Arphaxad yelled out across the pier: "May I tell you about the innate goodness of man?"

The speaker was obviously pleased that someone, anyone, had carefully listened to the first part of his speech. "Why, yes, young fellow, I believe I would like to hear about the innate goodness of man, and I believe that all these dear people would also like to hear you. Come on up." With that invitation, the ex-thug and his friend Enoch scampered along the pier, leaped onto the ship, and joined the speaker on the forward deck. Many of the listeners on the docks snickered when they recognized Arphaxad the thug climbing onto the boat.

Arphaxad looked around the expectant crowd, many of whom had familiar faces. "Hey, everybody, listen up. This is Arphaxad. You remember me. I used to be a thug." With the attention of the crowd firmly captured, Arphaxad boldly proclaimed: "Let me tell you how innately good I am. Until I met the One True God that this speaker has already spoken about, I was innately evil, a thug, a kidnapper, a murderer."

The original speaker started to wonder if it were such a good idea to invite Arphaxad up to speak as the ex-thug continued. "I was covetous, boastful, proud, blasphemous, disobedient, unthankful, unholy, without natural affection, a truce breaker, a false accuser, incontinent, and fierce." Arphaxad paused for a moment as his words hit home with full force upon the speaker and the audience. "But now, I am a new man. I have a new heart. I have become a child of God."

Many people in the crowd, familiar with Arphaxad's past exploits or even the victim of his violent past, gasped at Arphaxad's announcement. "I am now a child of God. God has forgiven me of all of my sins. I stand here before you now and ask each one of you whom I have offended in the past to forgive me."

An agonizing look overcame Arphaxad's face as he spoke to the crowd. Most people assumed that the ex-thug was just overcome with the emotion of the moment. Even Enoch did not realize that the gentle rocking motion of the ship moored at the pier was starting to make Arphaxad's stomach queasy. One of the people in the audience most amazed at Arphaxad's words was Captain Peleg, a crusty, foulmouthed, stump of a sea captain with a wooden stump below his left knee. Captain Peleg, who had purchased several slaves from Arphaxad in the past, was well acquainted with the old Arphaxad. But this new Arphaxad was very disquieting to Captain Peleg, who was shocked that anyone as rotten and filthy as Arphaxad could ever stand up in front of a crowd of people and tell them that he was now a child of God.

Captain Peleg himself had been having bad dreams lately. He felt as if somebody, who knows, maybe even Arphaxad's God, was really gripping his heart and convicting him about buying and shipping and selling slaves. Now, Arphaxad's preaching was stirring up those same bad dreams. The captain listened intently as Arphaxad continued.

With evident distress, Arphaxad kept preaching. "How bad was the innate Arphaxad? My sister, a wicked priestess of the cult of the Great Ebony Cow, paid me to kill a simple shepherd man. I went after that shepherd, bashed his head in with a shittim club, and then kidnapped his only daughter. Next, I sold his daughter into slavery to the most wicked captain on the seas -- Captain Blackheart."

The mention of the name of Captain Blackheart sent shivers down the back of many listeners. His reputation on the seas was worse than Arphaxad's reputation on land. The crowd knew that death and destruction always followed in Captain Blackheart's wake. Strangely, no one could recall seeing Captain Blackheart for the last couple of years.

The crowd's thoughts went back to Arphaxad as he kept telling his testimony. "But God has forgiven me of all of my murderous, malicious deeds. In fact, our miracle-working God even spared the life of that poor shepherd man whose head I had bashed in. That shepherd man has forgiven me for all of the evil deeds which I wrought against him and his family."

Captain Peleg, among many others in the audience, could not believe Arphaxad's last comment. He yelled out: "Get off it, Arphaxad, you old thug. You are just telling us a sailor's story. No father would ever forgive you for kidnapping his daughter and selling her into slavery!"

Arphaxad just gleamed when he recognized the scorner. "Ah, Captain Peleg, my old friend. I am so glad that you made that firm statement. Let me introduce you and the rest of the audience to that very shepherd man." With a flourish, Arphaxad pivoted toward his traveling companion and yelled to the crowd: "I present to you Enoch, a shepherd and a prophet of God."

All eyes turned toward the lean, blond, blue-eyed man standing on the forward deck next to the ex-thug. As soon as Enoch opened his mouth, Arphaxad beat a quick retreat off of the rocking ship onto the security and stability of the pier. "Dear friends," Enoch started, "everything which Arphaxad has told you is true. Arphaxad did bash my head in, he did kidnap my only daughter, and then he sold her into slavery to Captain Blackheart." Everyone immediately felt sorry for the poor man as a tear started to form in his eye and as his voice started to crack. "At first, I was just glad to be alive. At first, I hated Arphaxad. But my hatred was turned into a longing, not just to find my little girl, but also to find the God of the universe Who holds all things together by the power of His hand. I then set out searching for the God of the universe. Amazingly, I finally found Him, or rather, God found me."

Enoch's talk of such a personal God gripped the hearts of many listeners, including Captain Peleg. "The God of the universe loved me and forgave me of all of my sins when I turned my heart toward Him. Then, and only then, was I able to forgive Arphaxad for all of the evil which he had done to me."

Enoch paused and turned toward the strangely-garbed foreign philosopher who was still standing on the forward deck with Enoch. "Man is not innately good, but rather innately evil. I am innately evil. Arphaxad is innately evil. And this philosopher up here with me on this ship is innately evil." The philosopher gulped and took a step or two backward as Enoch continued. "All of us are sinners. And the wages of sin is death, that is, separation from God. One day the coming Redeemer shall come with ten thousands of His saints to execute judgment upon all that are ungodly among them of all their ungodly deeds."

Enoch's words cut deeply into the heart of Captain Peleg. He knew that he was a sinner. He knew that selling people into slavery did not please God. He wanted to run away from the voice of God's prophet, but some unseen force seemed to plant his shoes to the dock. Enoch's words kept pressing harder and harder into his heart. "If you people, from this fair city and from all the lands of the Earth, shall humble yourselves, and pray, and seek God's face, and turn from your wicked ways, then will God hear from Heaven and He will forgive you your sin."

The hope of forgiveness and freedom from the bondage of sin was a ray of sunlight in Captain Peleg's sin-darkened heart. Almost unconsciously the captain's lips opened and he cried out: "Sirs, what must I do to be saved?"

Enoch quickly scanned the audience and identified the speaker. Then Enoch turned to find Arphaxad, who was sitting on the pier next to the ship. Enoch motioned with his eyes for Arphaxad to go deal with the man who was seeking the Lord. Then, Enoch very simply answered Captain Peleg's question: "Believe on the coming Redeemer, and thou shalt be saved."

Captain Peleg fell to his knees as if someone had knocked him down. In a moment Arphaxad was at his side, putting his arm around the old sea captain; right there, in the midst of the milling crowd, Arphaxad led Captain Peleg to a saving knowledge of the coming Redeemer.

While Arphaxad dealt with the sea captain, the philosopher quietly slipped off of the ship and disappeared into the crowd. Enoch kept the people's attention as he told them that anyone who comes to God must come to God as a little child, believing that God really does exist, that God loves us but hates sin, that God must punish sin and cannot permit sin to spoil Heaven, and that if we trust in the coming Redeemer to cleanse us of all our sins, He will save us from our sins and make us a child of God.

The crowd then marveled when both Arphaxad and Captain Peleg stood up, both of them with tears in their eyes as they hugged each other. Then Captain Peleg walked with Arphaxad back to the ship. Arphaxad politely let Captain Peleg board first, then Arphaxad sat down again on the pier. Captain Peleg gave Enoch a big hug and then asked the prophet of God if he could say a few words.

"This here is Captain Peleg. Most of you folks know that I am a man of few words, and most of those few words I can't even repeat right now." A few people laughed as Captain Peleg kept talking. "I don't rightly understand everything that just happened to me here at the docks, except that I do know that God just saved my soul from sin and made me His child. I really can't explain it, but I sure do want as many of you as possible to come on board this here ship and let my new brothers Enoch and Arphaxad explain to you how you, too, can become a child of God." Then, Captain Peleg could speak no more as tears rolled down his cheeks.

Revival broke out in the docks. All four of Captain Peleg's ship hands came on board and were led to the Lord by either Enoch or Arphaxad. Sailors from other ships as well as numerous city dwellers from the City of Shorr came forward and trusted in the coming Redeemer. As each sailor made a profession of faith, Enoch encouraged him to take the good news of the coming Redeemer back home to his native land and to every port of call. Enoch was overcome with the power of God to spread the good news around the world.

## Chapter Forty

# Grow Where You Are Planted

Enoch and Arphaxad faithfully discipled each and every one of the new converts among the sailors and city dwellers of the City of Shorr, spending several weeks in numerous studies of the Words of God and teaching them many of the songs of God. The City of Shorr had never witnessed such a continual outpouring of the Spirit of God. Enoch lost track of time as the days, then weeks, of God's multiplied blessings rolled by.

One day Enoch came to Arphaxad in a very excited state. "My brother, have I ever got some great news!"

"Some more people trusted in the Lord, Enoch?" Arphaxad asked.

"Even better!" Enoch replied enthusiastically. "Captain Peleg has offered to carry you and me across the ocean to preach the good news. God has really convicted him about the slave trade. He wants to transport liberty from now on, liberty that only comes from trusting in the coming Redeemer. Arphaxad, Captain Peleg feels led of God to ferry us from port to port so we can preach the good news to so many multiplied thousands of people."

Arphaxad was not so excited. “You’re not getting me on one of those ocean voyages, Enoch, and that’s final.”

Enoch was as stubborn as Arphaxad. “Where’s your faith, my friend?”

“Right here on God’s good earth, not out in the middle of some fool ocean,” Arphaxad insisted.

“You better pray about your attitude, Arphaxad,” Enoch angrily snapped.

“You, too!” Arphaxad replied harshly, as he stormed off the pier and headed toward the house of one of the new converts. That night Enoch decided that he would sleep on Captain Peleg’s ship, to be closer to his dream of traveling even farther with the good news.

The sea was very rough that night, keeping Enoch up long after Captain Peleg and his crew fell asleep in their bunks. Enoch never knew that the sea could be so rough while the ship was just resting at harbor. The prophet left the sleeping quarters and went up to the deck, which swayed to and fro under his feet in the pounding wind which stirred up the waves. Enoch leaned on the rail, looked up at the moon, and complained to the Lord: “Lord, Arphaxad is just not growing as an evangelist. He seems to be resisting the wonderful opportunity to spread the good news even farther around the world.” Then Enoch asked the Lord: “Lord, don’t you want Arphaxad and me to go to the ends of the Earth? Or Lord, do you want me to travel with Captain Peleg and leave my dear friend Arphaxad behind? Lord, I just don't know what to do."

Then, to Enoch's utter amazement, the Lord appeared out on the water, standing securely on the billowing waves. Enoch, who nearly fell overboard from surprise, fell to his knees and humbled himself upon the deck. The Lord then spoke to His prophet: "Come to Me, Enoch."

Enoch was as stunned by the Lord's words as he was by the Lord's presence. "But-but Lord, I can't walk on the waves."

"Where's your faith, My friend?" the Lord gently rebuked.

Enoch was humbled by the Lord's words, the same words which Enoch had spoken earlier that evening when arguing with Arphaxad. "Forgive me, Lord, for arguing with Arphaxad."

"I forgive you, son. Now, come to Me."

"Are You sure You want me out in those big waves, Lord?"

The Lord was patient. "Come to Me, Enoch."

Finally, Enoch realized that the Lord was really serious. Instead of just jumping off of the ship, Enoch climbed over the railing and hesitantly lowered one foot toward the water. When that foot got wet, Enoch quickly raised it out of the water. "It's wet out there, Lord."

Enoch heard God laugh. "Enoch, just jump feet first into the water."

Enoch felt rather foolish in his lack of faith. Nonetheless, as he finally obeyed the Lord and leaped feet first toward the water, the courageous man of God closed his eyes in stark terror.

For the second time in as many minutes, Enoch was utterly amazed. When his feet hit the water, he did not sink. Although Captain Peleg's ship continued to rock back and forth in the rough winds, Enoch stood firm, as on a rock. "Come to Me, Enoch," the Lord repeated.

Enoch finally opened his eyes and looked straight at the Lord. "Look at Me, Enoch. Do not take your eyes off of Me for even one moment."

Enoch fixed his eyes on the Lord's eyes as the traveling evangelist took his first hesitant step. Enoch was utterly amazed again as he started to walk on the water toward his awaiting Lord.

Just then, the wind became more boisterous and the waves seemed to rise up higher than before. For a moment, Enoch took his eyes off of the Lord as he looked down at the mounting waves. At that very moment, with his eyes off of the Lord and onto the immediate danger which he faced, Enoch began to sink. He started waving his arms as he cried out: "Lord, save me!"

Before Enoch's knees got wet, the Lord stretched forth His mighty arm and caught Enoch's flailing right hand. "O ye of little faith," the Lord spoke as He lifted Enoch up to stand at His side. Then the Lord walked with Enoch, hand in hand, back to Captain Peleg's ship. When they reached the side of the ship, the Lord and Enoch just levitated into the air until their feet were firmly on deck. Immediately, the wind ceased.

With his feet back on deck, Enoch regained his courage. "Lord, I have a wonderful opportunity to preach the good news to the uttermost parts of the Earth."

"Yes, I know," said the Lord dryly.

"Isn't that exciting?" Enoch bubbled. "But Lord, it seems like Arphaxad does not want to go with me. Do You want me to go without him?"

The Lord looked sternly at Enoch, whose enthusiasm began to dry up under the Lord's withering stare. "Did I say something wrong, Lord?" Enoch meekly asked.

"Enoch," the Lord reminded, "did I not promise you that I would raise up a traveling companion for you?"

"Why, yes, Lord."

"And did I not keep My promise, Enoch?"

"Yes, Lord."

"Then why do you want to thwart My will?"

Enoch gulped. "But Lord, what have I done?"

The Lord glared at His prophet. "Why are you trying to get rid of the traveling companion which I raised up for you?"

Enoch became even more confused. "B-B-But Lord, Arphaxad doesn't want to travel overseas with me to preach Your good news."

"Have you discerned My will on that matter, Enoch?" the Lord questioned.

"Well, not exactly, Lord, but Captain Peleg offered the use of his ship and crew, and it really seems like a wonderful idea."

"No, Enoch," the Lord firmly responded, "it is not My will. You and Arphaxad are not to travel overseas."

Enoch's heart sank faster than his feet did moments earlier on the waves. His thoughts turned to all of the people who needed to hear the good news of the coming Redeemer. The Lord then answered Enoch's thoughts: "One of your descendants, Enoch, shall travel overseas, indeed to the uttermost parts of the Earth, to preach the good news."

Then Enoch's thoughts turned toward the subject which he really did not want to admit to his Lord -- he wanted to search for his daughter Crista. Again the Lord could hear Enoch's thoughts. "Enoch, your motives for traveling overseas are tainted by selfish desires. Wherever you go, it should be for the sole purpose of preaching the good news."

Enoch lowered his eyes and wept bitterly as he finally admitted the sin in his heart. "Lord," Enoch sobbed, "it was wrong for me to use Crista as a reason for going overseas. I am truly sorry. Please forgive me, Lord."

The Lord looked tenderly at His prophet and knew that the prophet of God was truly earnest in his confession. Before the Lord could respond, Enoch continued his confession. "And Lord, it was wrong for me to worry about Crista. I believe that You will restore her to me in Your timing. I'm sorry, Lord. Would You please forgive me?"

"Yes, My child, I forgive you. You will have many wonderful ideas how to preach the good news to so many people. But even more important than good ideas is obedience to the known will of God."

"Yes, my Lord," Enoch humbly replied.

"Enoch, you know that it is My will that Arphaxad be your traveling companion. If any of your ideas would lead you away from traveling with Arphaxad, then you know that that idea is not from Me."

"Yes, my Lord."

"One final thing, Enoch. You also know, although you may have forgotten in your excitement over the revival here in the City of Shorr, that you and Arphaxad must be back home exactly six months to the day from when you last left your homestead. The six months is almost up, Enoch. You and your traveling companion must hurry home to meet My deadline."

"Oh, Lord, I had almost forgotten," Enoch quickly confessed. "Oh, I am so sorry, Lord. I guess I get carried away sometimes."

"Enoch, you must always seek to get carried away -- carried away in the Spirit of God.

I am pleased with you, son, that My name has been glorified here in the City of Shorr. Rest assured, Enoch, that the good news will be spread across the world by the sailors who have become believers here in this city. Get a good night's rest, My son; then you and Arphaxad need to head out early in the morning."

As the Lord departed, a heavy sleep fell over Enoch, who spent the rest of the night huddled on the deck, right where the Lord had been standing. For some reason, the deck exuded a warmth which kept Enoch warm all night long.

Early in the morning, Captain Peleg found the prophet of God fast asleep topside. "Enoch, Enoch, wake up. Are you all right?"

Enoch wrestled with the sudden noise ringing in his ears. As he opened his eyes, he saw the rather ugly face of Captain Peleg staring down at him. "Good morning, Captain," Enoch replied groggily.

"What are you doing out here on the deck?" the captain asked gruffly.

"I met with the Lord here last night, Captain Peleg."

"On board my ship?" the captain asked in amazement.

"Yes, Captain. Right here. The Lord told me that Arphaxad and I must return home immediately."

"The Lord was here on my ship?" Captain Peleg repeated again.

"Yes, sir, Captain. I must thank you for your generous offer to take me to faraway lands to preach the good news, but the Lord has other plans for Arphaxad and me."

Just then Arphaxad appeared on the dock. "Good morning, Enoch. Good morning, Captain Peleg. Hey, Enoch, I really must apologize for yelling at you last night. Can you forgive me?"

Before Enoch could answer, Captain Peleg yelled out loud: "Arphaxad, the Lord was here on my ship last night."

Arphaxad immediately looked at the prophet of God. "Is that right, Enoch?"

"Yes, my brother. The Lord met me here last night aboard this ship."

"What did He say to you, Enoch?" Arphaxad eagerly questioned.

"The Lord told me that He does not want you and me to travel overseas."

"Praise the Lord!" shouted the relieved traveling companion. "God has truly answered my prayers."

Enoch just smiled at his friend. "And Arphaxad, we must leave early this morning to return home. Remember -- we are supposed to be home six months to the day from when we last left home."

Captain Peleg then interrupted. "Men, I am so honored that God has set foot on my ship. This ship is now sanctified to His glory. Before you two head out, please eat a hearty breakfast with me and my crew. Then, I will give you my blessing before you travel."

Arphaxad was mighty glad to hear all the good news. "Well, Enoch, we will soon be on the road again -- together."

# Part Four

# Showdown at the Temple of Gom

721 A.C.

## Chapter Forty-one

# Bad News

Enoch's spirits were soaring as he and Arphaxad approached Enoch's homestead in the middle of the afternoon on the day that was exactly six months to the day when the traveling evangelists had departed. Enoch so looked forward to seeing Methuselah and Elihu and especially Sarah. How dearly he missed them when he was on the road, even though Arphaxad was probably the best fellow traveler in the world. Enoch was eager to share the wonderful stories of the Great Sea and the City of Shorr and the mighty revival which started there and was spreading throughout the world.

"Enoch," Arphaxad asked, interrupting his friend's reverie, "why do you think the Lord wanted us back home on this day?"

"Hard to say, my friend," Enoch answered. "The Lord must have had a good reason for telling us to return today, and He must have had a good reason for not telling us why."

As the road north looped east and neared Enoch's homestead by the tamarisk grove, Enoch just smiled and said: "I just can't wait to get home, kick off these shoes, put my feet up, and drink a tall glass of fresh orange juice."

Arphaxad chuckled: "Maybe you ought to wash your feet first, my friend." Just then, eagle-eyed Arphaxad spotted the familiar grove of tamarisk trees in the distance. "We are almost home!" The two men unconsciously and simultaneously picked up their pace at the sight of the homestead landmark. As they neared the grove, Arphaxad was surprised by an unexpected sound: "Enoch, doesn't that sound like a horse neighing?"

Enoch heard the sound, too. His heart beat a little faster as the two men walked even faster, then started to jog toward the grove. As they reached the top of the hill and looked down at the homestead, they both saw Elam's horse and wagon. "What is Elam doing at the house?" Enoch thought to himself.

Standing next to the horse were three men -- Methuselah, Elihu, and Ludim. "Ludim?" Enoch spoke aloud. "What's going on? What kind of reception committee is this? Where's Elam?" Just then, Elihu spotted the two traveling evangelists at the top of the hill. "They're home! They're home!"

As Elihu and Methuselah started running up the hill, the front door burst open. With a sigh of relief, Sarah, too, began to dash up the hill. Ludim stayed with the horse, apparently rechecking the reins. Enoch could hear Elihu yell to Methuselah: "Your mother was right, Methuselah. They did return home today!"

Methuselah hugged his father first. "Oh, Dad, I am so glad you are home!" Then Elihu, then Sarah all started hugging the returning travelers. "I just knew you would make it home in time, Enoch."

Enoch's joy at being reunited with his family was mixed with feelings of unease. As everyone finally walked down the hill and neared Elam's horse and wagon, Enoch asked: "Is Elam here?"

Then, Ludim walked over and gave a bearhug to Enoch and Arphaxad. "You men have arrived just in time. Hop in the wagon. We must hurry!"

Arphaxad looked down at the anxious blacksmith. "Whoa! Don't we get a welcome home feast first?"

"There is no time for that, Arphaxad. We must hurry into Gom."

Enoch could not understand what was going on. "Sarah, what is going on? Where is Elam? Why should we rush into Gom? I'm kind of tired. I would like to kick off these shoes, put my feet up, and drink a tall glass of orange juice."

"Enoch," said Sarah impatiently, "I have packed up a bag of biscuits. I will get you a glass of orange juice. But then you and Arphaxad must speed into Gom with Ludim."

Enoch couldn't stand the suspense any longer. "Wait a minute, everybody. Someone has to tell me what's going on."

Ludim looked over at Sarah, who looked over at Methuselah, who looked over at Elihu. When no one's eyes met Enoch's, the prophet of God said in frustration: "Is the Lord going to have to tell me?"

Finally, Ludim spoke up. "Surely, you and Arphaxad have heard about the dedication service in the City of Gom today!"

"What dedication service?" Enoch quizzed.

"You don't know, Enoch?" Ludim quizzed in return.

"No, I don't !" he replied with impatience. "Arphaxad and I have been hundreds of miles south of here, all the way to the City of Shorr and the Great Sea. We haven't heard any news from these parts in months. But, boy, do Arphaxad and I have some great news from the City of Shorr."

"No time for that, Enoch. There is only bad news here in the City of Gom."

Enoch's eagerness to share the good news of the great revival in the City of Shorr was being dampened by the mood of the reception committee. "All right. All right!" he exclaimed. "Tell me about this dedication service in Gom."

"Enoch, I knew you would be home today," Sarah interrupted. "That's why I have the bag of biscuits ready for you and Arphaxad to eat while you rush into town."

Enoch just smiled at his wife as she handed him the bag of biscuits and hustled him into the wagon. Then Sarah continued: "You must stop the dedication ceremony before it is too late, Enoch." Sarah gave Enoch a good-bye kiss as Ludim and Arphaxad also climbed into the wagon. As Arphaxad reached for the bag of biscuits, Enoch asked one final time: "Sarah, before we head out, could you just tell me what is being dedicated in Gom today?"

Sarah stopped all motion, looked straight into Enoch's eyes, and gravely pronounced: "Enoch, while you and Arphaxad were gone, Zaava and Tubal built a temple to the Great Ebony Cow right in the middle of the City of Gom."

Enoch rose from the wagon seat. "What!?! I can't believe it! Here in Gom!?!"

"Yes, dear," Sarah breathlessly continued. "This afternoon, High Priest Cain will himself dedicate the new temple."

"Cain!?! Here in Gom? What madness!"

"You must hurry, Enoch. Elam desperately wants you to stop the dedication service."

"Where is Elam, Sarah?"

"Ludim took him home yesterday. That is why Ludim is here with Elam's horse and wagon."

Enoch looked over at his friend. Ludim was eager to start the long ride into town. "We really must get going, Enoch."

Sarah started to weep. "Enoch, you must save Adah's baby."

"Hold it, Ludim," Enoch ordered. "Sarah, what's this about Adah and a baby?"

"Enoch, Adah had a baby, and Cain is going to, to, to . . ."

"Cain is going to do what, Sarah?"

Sarah caught her breath, and through her tears cried: "Cain is going to dedicate the Temple of Gom with the sacrifice of Adah's baby."

Without looking back, without waving to his wife, to his son, or to Elihu, Enoch barked a command: "Let's ride!"

## Chapter Forty-two

# Elam's Distress

Ludim whipped Elam's horse at a punishing pace as the three men hurried along the road to the City of Gom. Arphaxad, who had been sitting in the back of Elam's wagon eating several of Sarah's biscuits, finally yelled at the blacksmith: "You will kill the horse if you keep running him like this!"

Ludim whipped the horse another time: "Better that the horse die than Adah's baby." As the horse and wagon and riders sped down the road, Enoch asked his friend: "How did all of this come about?"

Ludim was relieved to finally tell the story to his friend. Arphaxad could hear every word as the wind whipped the blacksmith's voice behind him. "It seems like the very day that you and Arphaxad left on your last journey, a strange building project started at the marketplace near the city fountain. Tubal acted as the chief builder, with Aram as his assistant."

Enoch winced at his brother's name. A dark feeling spread over the prophet's soul as the blacksmith continued his story. "No one knew what was being built, but over a hundred men from faraway cities were quickly putting together a pretty big foundation. I finally went and talked to my son, but Tubal refused to see me."

Enoch could see tears form in the bulky blacksmith's eyes as he whipped the horse again. "Everyone in town wondered what was being built, but no one who knew would tell the people. We all watched the foundation being laid and the walls going up. Finally, Rekim, Fallon, and I went together in the middle of the day to confront Tubal."

"Did he finally talk to you?"

"He still refused to tell me what he was building. All he said was that the building would bring great fame and honor to the City of Gom and that he was securing his financial future by building the large structure." Ludim's tears flowed again as he thought of the greed that consumed his son. As the road rounded a sharp turn, Ludim didn't even slow down, expertly shifting his weight and steering the horse as he continued to tell the story to the momentarily frightened evangelists. "Then, last week, Tubal and Zaava appeared at the south gate to make an announcement to the city. Tubal announced that the nearly completed structure near the city fountain was nothing less than the newest and most exotic Temple of the Great Ebony Cow. Even as he spoke, the ebony cow from Zaava's house was paraded up and down the marketplace. Then Tubal introduced Zaava, my daughter-in-law, God curse her name, as the great high priestess of the Temple of Gom."

Ludim spat out of the wagon as he mentioned Zaava's name. "Zaava was wearing this outrageously provocative costume. Then she started to speak. I couldn't believe my ears, Enoch."

"What did she say, Ludim?"

"She said that High Priest Cain himself, the founder of the City of Cain and of the cult of the Great Ebony Cow, would personally visit the City of Gom to dedicate the new temple. I just about threw up, Enoch. But most of the other people in the marketplace started cheering at the mention of Cain's name. Maybe God just ought to destroy the whole city."

"We live in terrible times, my friend."

"It gets worse, Enoch," the blacksmith continued. "Just eight days ago, Elam's daughter Adah had a baby. Somehow, word of the birth of the baby leaked out and reached Elam. He decided that he wanted to see his grandchild. Yesterday, Elam drove into town with this horse and wagon."

Arphaxad spoke up from the back of the wagon. "Did Elam get to see his grandbaby?"

"Just a few hours before Elam showed up in town, there was a grand procession that went by my blacksmith shop near the north gate of the city. One hundred armed priests of the cult of the Great Ebony Cow rode into town on black horses.

Right in the middle of the procession, in a grand golden carriage, rode Cain himself. Incredibly, many of the people alongside the main road bowed to the ground as Cain went by. The procession made its way to Zaava's house, which was specially appointed to take care of Cain and his contingent."

"That's a murderous group," Arphaxad added. "I would hate to mess with them."

"Then Elam came into town. He rode past the new temple and first came to my blacksmith shop. Oh, Enoch, I had never seen Elam look worse from worry about his little girl and his grandchild. He told me that he knew it was fruitless to try to get his daughter Adah to come home with him, but he thought he would try to gain custody of his grandchild. The man looked so pitiful, Enoch, when I told him that Cain and one hundred armed priests were now holed up at Zaava's house and that the Temple of Gom was going to be dedicated the next day."

"What did Elam do?"

"He asked me if I would ride with him to Zaava's house. The poor man -- he didn't even know how to get there. So I rode in the same seat you are riding in, Enoch, as Elam slowly drove his horse, the same one I am running to death now, up to Zaava's house."

Arphaxad groaned. "Elam wouldn't stand a chance with all of Cain's guards there."

"Elam told me to stay in the wagon while he went up to the front door. Several of Cain's guards were stationed at the door. They asked Elam what he wanted. Then one of them went inside for a minute, and returned quickly, escorting Elam inside. I could not believe that he would gain entrance into Zaava's house. Later, Elam told me, with difficulty, what happened inside."

"Well," Arphaxad asked eagerly, "what happened next?"

"The guards led Elam into the Great Chamber. There, sitting underneath that stupid ebony cow, was Cain, with Zaava at his side. Cain thundered at Zaava: 'Who is this miserable cur?' Zaava told Cain that the pitiful looking man was Elam, Adah's father. Before anyone else could say anything, Elam boldly proclaimed: 'Give me my grandchild!'"

"Cain just laughed. 'That would be quite impossible, Elam. I have very special plans for your grandchild.'"

"Elam had no sense of intimidation as he requested again: 'Let me see my grandchild.'"

"Cain chuckled and ordered Zaava to bring in Adah and the baby. Just a few moments later Adah was brought in, holding her baby in her arms. Elam cried out to his daughter, who was too ashamed to even look at her father. Cain then ordered Adah to kiss the mark of Cain. While her father looked on with disbelief, Adah walked over and kissed Cain on the forehead. Then Cain proudly proclaimed: 'Adah is no longer your daughter, Elam. Now she is mine!'"

"Elam cried out to Adah. A guard then struck Elam in the mouth. As blood poured out of Elam's mouth, Cain ordered Adah to hand him the baby. Adah meekly handed her baby to the old, evil man. Cain cradled the baby in his arms and announced to Elam: 'And this baby is not your granddaughter. The baby is mine.'"

"That was the first that Elam had heard whether his grandbaby was a boy or a girl. Elam shrieked and lunged toward his grandchild. Two guards grabbed him and threw him roughly to the floor. Cain looked down at the bruised and broken man. 'Look one more time, Elam, at your granddaughter. You will never see her again. Tomorrow I shall sacrifice her at the dedication of the Temple of the Great Ebony Cow.' Then, Adah shrieked: 'No! My baby! My baby! Don't kill my baby!' As Adah reached for her baby, Zaava grabbed her by the arms and held her back. Adah wept uncontrollably as Cain ordered two guards to return Adah to her room, alone. Elam once again tried to rise, but a guard slapped him down again. 'Toss that miserable cur out of here!' Cain ordered. Two guards then picked up the distraught father and grandfather, carried him to the front door, and then threw him down the steps."

Enoch grimaced from the awful story. "Poor Elam. Poor Adah."

Just then, the wagon ascended the hill overlooking the City of Gom. “We are almost there, Enoch,” Ludim shouted excitedly. Ludim whipped the horse again as the wagon crested the hill. Greeting them was an ominous sign -- a thread of smoke was ascending from the center of the City of Gom.

## Chapter Forty-three

# The Temple of Gom

The wagon screamed down the hill. As they neared the south gate, they saw a woman motioning them to stop and pull off of the road. "That's Perna," Ludim yelled as he brought the horse to a stop. The three men leaped out of the wagon and ran to Perna, who was just outside of the city gate.

"It's too late, Ludim," Perna shared with tears streaming down her face. All three men lowered their heads and grieved over the life of the little one. Ludim hugged his wife and gently comforted her: "Adah's baby is in a better place now."

Tears flowed down Enoch's face as he struggled over the loss of such an innocent life, yet grateful for the believer's blessed hope.

Arphaxad, too, was tearful. "I guess we lost the race for life, Enoch. I hate to lose anything to Cain. What do we do now?"

"I don't know, my friend. God will direct our paths. First, let's say a prayer, not for the little one, but for Adah, and for Elam, and for Aram, and for all of the confused, beguiled people of the City of Gom." There, outside the city gate of the City of Gom, while a celebration of death was going on inside the city, four believers in the One True God held a prayer meeting, safe in the arms of the Lord of life.

After prayer, Ludim asked Perna about Cain and his guards. "Cain and all of his guards are at the temple, Ludim. Cain is so confident in his show of force that he did not even leave any guards at the city gates."

Enoch's eyes lit up. Arphaxad alone caught the gleam in his friend's eyes. "We are in trouble now," Arphaxad exclaimed.

Ludim jerked toward Arphaxad and asked breathlessly: "What's wrong? Do you see any of Cain's guards?"

"Worse," Arphaxad explained. "Enoch has an idea."

Ludim and Perna glanced over at Enoch, who seemed lost in thought. "What are you thinking of, Enoch?" Ludim demanded.

Enoch's brow was furled. "If Cain did not leave any guards at the city gates, he must either think that Arphaxad and I will not show up or that we are no match for his one hundred armed priestly guards. If we can catch Cain off guard, then maybe we can put a stop to their celebration of death."

"Well," Arphaxad quizzed, "what do you plan to do?"

"I still don't know, but I do know that we will find out the answer inside the city." With that said, Enoch started to walk, quietly and without fanfare, through the south gate. His friends had no choice but to follow.

What Enoch saw astounded him -- right in the middle of the main street, right next to the city fountain, rose a square building thirty feet high, with six pillars on each side. Seen through the pillars on the east side of the temple was a large black statue of a cow. Enoch almost chuckled at the thought that normal, sane, reasonable human beings would even think of the idea of worshipping such a ridiculous symbol. But then, Enoch saw, right in the middle of the temple, a brazen altar from which smoke and the stench of death was rising into the late afternoon sky.

All heads were facing the temple; no one was looking back toward the south city gate where four newcomers slowly approached the crowd. Then, Enoch was able to see two men, one tall and one short, standing on either side of the brazen altar. Enoch quickly recognized the shorter of the two men -- Lalomar. Even though he was wearing a black robe with the hood up, Enoch could make out Lalomar's peculiar features. The other priestly figure was not moving about, and Enoch could not peer through the hood. "Who is the other priest?" Enoch whispered to Perna.

"Aram."

Enoch had to stifle a scream. "Oh, no, Lord, not my brother!" God's prophet cried inside to Heaven. "Spare him, Father. Please spare him."

As they moved in a little closer, Enoch could see several figures sitting underneath the Great Ebony Cow. "Cain!" Enoch thought to himself. Sitting on either side of Cain, in much smaller chairs, were Zaava and Adah. While Zaava looked radiant, exultant, majestic, poor Adah looked like she had just lost her best friend.

Surrounding the entire temple were Cain's guards, twenty-five on each side of the temple. Surrounding the guards were the jammed throngs of city dwellers, all eager to be close to Cain and his newest temple. As the smoke from the altar began to die out, Cain snapped his fingers. Then Zaava stood up, and with every eye watching, yelled out: "Let the feast begin!"

While the three men and one woman looked on with amazement, dozens of roast cow were brought up to the temple by Zaava's servants and placed on tables that suddenly appeared from nowhere, encircling the temple. The gathered crowd, like ravishing animals, all struggled to get near the tables of free roast cow.

Then, Enoch saw his brother inside the temple grab a hammer and strike at some object within the temple. The sound of the city gong reverberated throughout the city. Enoch and Arphaxad quickly turned to look at the east platform of the city gate. Indeed, the city gong was gone from its familiar position. "The city people donated the city gong to Cain's new temple," Ludim explained.

Enoch was aghast at how completely the city had welcomed Cain's new temple. As the sound of the gong ceased, Zaava raised her arms and proclaimed to the crowd: "Before we eat, let us first give thanks for this wonderful feast." Then Zaava turned toward the statue and lifted her eyes and arms: "O Great Ebony Cow, most visible and most high god, we praise you for your goodness and your love toward all of these wonderful people of the City of Gom."

Arphaxad smirked: "They really showed a lot of goodness and love toward Adah's poor baby."

Zaava continued: "We praise you that you have kept our enemies from us today. Strike dead those enemies of the Great Ebony Cow before they can do us any harm."

Arphaxad leaned over to Enoch. "I think she means us, my friend."

Zaava then concluded her short prayer. "We thank you for providing all of this delicious meat for all of these wonderful people of Gom. O Great Ebony Cow, bless this temple to your matchless glory. Amen!"

Enoch listened intently to Zaava's prayer. He now knew what God wanted him to do. Without saying a word, Enoch quietly retreated back toward the south gate, followed by his three friends. "Where are you going, Enoch? You aren't running away from this, are you?"

"Follow me," Enoch softly replied as he led the small group of believers up the steps of the east platform. As the sun sank lower and lower in the western sky, Enoch surveyed the scene at the temple. Thousands of city dwellers were clawing and scratching and fighting to get near the tables of free food. Enoch wanted to get the attention of the city dwellers, and he knew that only a very loud noise would get their attention. But the gong was gone.

Enoch lifted his head Heavenward and prayed aloud: "Most gracious God, the Only True God, let Your light so shine before men, that they may see Your good works, that You and You alone may be glorified. Until the Redeemer comes, Amen!"

Then, Enoch raised the staff of God and waved it over his head.

## Chapter Forty-four

# Enoch's Challenge

The twilight sky momentarily became as noonday as a bolt of light streaked through the air with a loud, rumbling sound. All activity and all voices ceased near the temple as every eye turned toward the east platform.

Zaava and Lalomar were enraged at this sudden interruption of Zaava's glorious celebration. Cain himself sat smiling, contented behind the protection of one hundred guards and eager for another opportunity to rid the world of that pestilent prophet. Cain leaned over toward the flustered Zaava and calmly asked: "Didn't you say that we should not expect to see this mad prophet? Didn't I tell you that we should make every precaution for his sudden arrival?"

Zaava gritted her teeth. "Master Cain, I have had my spies out for more than a week all over the countryside. Even as late as this morning, my spies informed me that Enoch had not returned to this region. I just don't know where he came from."

"Dear Zaava, just make sure that he does not spoil the dedication of my new temple."

Aram's reaction to the sudden appearance of Enoch was unlike the others. A sense of dread filled the younger brother of God's prophet. His worst fears were being realized -- a confrontation with his own brother.

Adah's reaction to the unscheduled visitor was that of astonishment that her father's friend, that anyone would so openly oppose the dreadful Cain. She listened with quickened ears as the prophet of God began to speak.

"Your iniquity, people of Gom, is before you. You have not heeded the Words of God in the past. Pay heed to the Words of God today."

"You permitted, then embraced meat eating. When you would not turn from that iniquity, sin spread like a leprosy throughout the city. Next, you permitted a slave market, then embraced slavery. Still, you would not heed the Words of God."

"You were warned years ago that some people were burning incense to other gods and were worshipping the works of their own hands. First, you permitted it. Now, you embrace it. You would not heed the Words of God."

"It is still not too late. God is not willing that any should perish. Turn from your wicked ways and walk with God. Turn from meat eating. Turn from slavery. Turn from worshipping other gods. Today, turn from child sacrifice. Turn back to the One True God."

The crowd was subdued as Enoch spoke. Although everyone listened, Enoch prayed most earnestly for the two young people most on his heart -- Aram and Adah. "It is not too late to depart from evil. God will forgive you of all of your sins. Draw nigh unto God, and He will draw nigh unto you."

Aram's heart was torn. He knew that his brother was sincere, but Enoch's way seemed old-fashioned, out of date, unprofitable. The young man's heart was upon riches, and he knew that his brother had none. How could Enoch ask him to turn from Tubal, his gracious benefactor?

Adah's heart was also torn. Enoch's words struck her deeply. She knew that she had fallen from grace, had fallen into a trap. But how could she get out? Could it really be true that God would forgive such a wicked young lady as herself? Would God really draw nigh unto her if she drew nigh unto God? For a moment, Enoch's words gave the young lady hope. But then Adah thought of her father, whom she had forsaken. My father could never forgive me, Adah thought, for leaving home. He could never forgive me for becoming a priestess under Zaava. But most of all, Adah thought, Daddy could never forgive me for the death, the tragic, unnecessary death of his granddaughter.

As Enoch finished speaking, every eye turned upon Cain to see how he would respond to the prophet of the so-called One True God. Cain was very relaxed, very confident as he stood up, turned toward the east platform, and replied: "Art thou Enoch that troubleth the people of Gom?" Cain's question was skillfully crafted to make light of Enoch's threat and to put Enoch on the defensive.

Enoch did not know how to respond to Cain's question. While every eye was upon him, the prophet of God closed his eyes and prayed for wisdom. God answered his prayer immediately. Enoch opened his eyes and answered: "It is not I who have troubled the people of Gom, but rather Zaava and Cain, who have forsaken the commandments of the One True God and have followed the deaf, dumb, and blind Great Ebony Cow."

The crowd murmured at such insolence toward the great Cain and his religion. Zaava was enraged. "I'll kill him."

But Cain remained calm, restraining Zaava with his softly spoken words. "Be calm, my dear Zaava. You need not kill him. My guards are quite equipped for that task." Then Cain returned his attention to Enoch. "My poor, dear deranged man," Cain spoke in his most condescending manner, "you speak of your God, but I do not see him."

The crowd roared at Cain's clever reply. Enoch ignored it and continued to exhort the people of Gom. "How long halt ye between two opinions? If the Lord be God, follow Him: but if the Great Ebony Cow be god, then follow it."

The crowd became quiet again, awaiting Cain's response. Then Cain spoke again. "My poor, demented man, how do you expect these dear people to follow an unknown, invisible god?"

The crowd roared again with approval of Cain's remark. Enoch, severely discouraged by the nonresponsiveness of the people of Gom, prayed again from the depths of his heart: "Lord, their hearts are so hardened. It's hopeless, Lord!"

Then Enoch heard the voice of the Lord speak to his heart: "Gird up thy loins and speak unto them all that I command thee: be not dismayed at their faces, lest I confound thee before them."

Enoch was humbled by the Lord's sharp rebuke and warning. He dropped to his knees suddenly. Ludim, Perna, and Arphaxad were bewildered by Enoch's seeming sudden lack of courage. The crowd laughed as it appeared that Enoch was beaten in a battle of words with Cain. Cain just glanced over at Zaava and smirked victoriously: "So much for the dumb Sheep Man."

Enoch prayed once again: "Forgive me, Lord, for my unbelief." Then, while every eye was upon him, the prophet of God raised himself up. Ludim turned to Arphaxad and hastily said: "What could Enoch now say to recapture the attention and the respect of the people?"

Arphaxad quickly replied: "I don't know, but God and Enoch have special ways of doing things."

Then Enoch opened his eyes and opened his mouth. His words thundered across the marketplace: "My God challenges Cain's god to a duel!"

## Chapter Forty-five

# The Useless Wooden Statue

Cain shuddered momentarily at Enoch's challenge, along with everyone else gathered around the Temple of Gom. All eyes turned from Enoch to Cain.

Cain was on the spot and he knew it. To not accept the challenge would show fear; to hesitate would show doubt. So Cain quickly arose from his throne, stuck his fist in the air toward Enoch, and declared: "Cain accepts the challenge."

Cain turned toward Zaava and commanded: "Come with me." They walked quickly through the guards and the curious crowd and headed toward the west platform of the south city gate. Cain strode confidently, belying his advanced age, up the steps to the west platform. When he and Zaava reached the platform, Cain majestically swerved and faced Enoch and his friends on the east platform. "State your challenge!" Cain declared.

Enoch looked over the crowd. Every eye was upon him as he issued his unique challenge: "Call ye on the name of your god, and I will call on the name of the Lord: and the God that answereth by fire, let him be God."

Everyone on the west platform, everyone near the temple, and everyone on the east platform except Enoch shivered. Ludim turned to Arphaxad and asked: "Does Enoch do things like this very often?"

"First time," replied Arphaxad, shaking his head.

Cain, not as familiar with the ways of Enoch, turned to Zaava: "What do you think, Zaava?"

"It's a trick, Cain!" Zaava answered. "Enoch has that magic staff of his."

Cain contemplated Zaava's comment, then turned to the waiting crowd: "What think ye of Enoch's challenge?"

All of the people, eager to witness a showdown, answered and said: "It is well spoken."

Cain knew that he was still on the spot. He knew that he could not back down; yet, was it a fair contest, he questioned, as long as Enoch had that magic staff? Finally, Cain knew how to respond. He would turn the tables on Enoch. "I accept your challenge -- on one condition."

The answer of Cain titillated the crowd. After pausing a suitable moment to build the excitement, Cain declared his condition: "I accept your challenge with the condition that you not use your magic staff."

The crowd immediately responded: "It is well spoken." Cain gleamed all over, confident that Enoch would not accept his condition.

With great chagrin, Cain heard Enoch's immediate response: "I accept Cain's condition." Cain shivered as Enoch handed the staff of God to Arphaxad. Every eye watched as Arphaxad carried the staff down the steps of the east platform and placed the staff of God in the middle of the main street, pointed toward the temple.

While every eye was upon Arphaxad, the ex-thug turned toward the crowd and exclaimed: "Let Cain first call upon the name of his god."

Cain had never before faced such a challenge. He was not sure how to proceed. He huddled with Zaava for a minute. "You know this Sheep Man better than I do. What do you think we should do?"

"I have never faced such a challenge before with you, Master Cain. All I know is that I hate the Sheep Man with all of my heart."

"Then, Zaava, you should first call upon the name of the Great Ebony Cow."

Zaava did not fear the staff-less Sheep Man nor believed in his God. As all eyes watched the two figures on the west platform, Zaava turned toward the figure of the Great Ebony Cow and bellowed across the marketplace: "O Great Ebony Cow, hear me, your devoted servant. This Sheep Man has mocked your most holy name. O Great Ebony Cow, send fire from above and strike the Sheep Man dead!"

The crowd froze from anticipation. Moments, then minutes passed. The crowd then became jittery as nothing appeared in the sky. Zaava herself began to sweat. More minutes passed. Finally, Cain whispered to Zaava: "Do something else."

Zaava then knew that the useless wooden statue of the Great Ebony Cow could not help her in the challenge. She dropped all pretense and prayed directly to her one true lord: "O Satan, most earthly father here below, your humble servant prostrates her soul in humble obedience to your perfect will."

The crowd murmured as they heard Zaava speak the name of Satan. They hushed as she continued to invoke the name of the dread lord of sin and death. "My heart is on fire for you, O Satan, the father of fire, as I face your enemies this evening. Send fiery darts of death, O great Satan, into Enoch's blasphemous heart. Let these people know that you, O great Satan, and you alone, are supreme upon all the Earth."

The crowd gasped as Zaava continued to invoke the name of the prince of darkness. They shuddered at what evil might befall poor Enoch. All eyes looked expectantly for fiery darts to shoot forth from the temple straight to the east platform to strike down the Sheep Man.

But nothing happened. The stillness of the temple bespoke the powerlessness of Cain's god. Zaava turned in anguish to Cain: "Why doesn't Satan answer?"

Cain, ever calm, sarcastically replied: "Your power is weak, Zaava."

"I shall try again," Zaava desperately responded.

"Forget it, dear," Cain said sharply. "Cut your losses. You tried and you failed. Don't try and fail again."

"But I can't let Enoch win!" Zaava groaned.

"Don't worry, Zaava. The Sheep Man won't win unless his God answers him with fire," Cain spoke confidently. "And Enoch is powerless without his magic staff."

Zaava was greatly comforted by Cain's final words. Then Cain turned to the crowd and humbled Zaava in front of all of the people of Gom. "Dear people of the great City of Gom, young Zaava is still inexperienced as a high priestess of the cult of the Great Ebony Cow. She has much to learn, if you will but put up with her for a few more years." Zaava's countenance was mortified at Cain's public rebuke. She was speechless as Cain continued to address the people.

"But let the challenge continue!" Cain paused long enough to allow the attention of the crowd to turn toward Enoch on the east platform. "Let Enoch call upon his God. After Enoch fails, then perhaps Cain shall show you some true power."

The crowd roared with approval, eager for the challenge to continue. Ludim turned toward

Enoch and exclaimed: “Enoch, that’s not fair. You shouldn’t let Cain have a second chance like that.”

Enoch turned momentarily toward his old friend and confidently replied: “That’s all right, my friend. Cain won’t get a second chance. Our God shall not fail.”

## Chapter Forty-six

# Enoch's Final Invitation

Every eye was upon the prophet of God. Every mind wondered if Enoch's God was more powerful than Cain's.

Enoch's eyes scanned the multitude below him. His heart grieved him that the children of Adam, like so many dumb sheep, had strayed so far from their Great Shepherd.

The heart of the prophet of God also grieved for poor Adah, seemingly trapped in a seductive web of sin from which there seemed no escape. Enoch's mind wondered how Adah's father would react if the judgment of God would consume her in just a few minutes. How much more grief could Elam bear? The loss of his granddaughter? The loss of his daughter?

Enoch's heart also went out to his brother Aram. Would the judgment of God consume him today as greed had already consumed the young man's heart? Enoch thought of his own father. Would Jared understand the judgment of God, or would he blame Enoch?

Enoch's mind raced with these thoughts as he looked out over the crowd, the expectant crowd, eager for excitement and action, eager for the conclusion of the showdown at the Temple of Gom.

"People of Gom," the prophet of God began, "I give you one final invitation, one more opportunity to turn back to the One True God. Depart, I pray, from the temple of these wicked people, and touch nothing of theirs, lest ye be consumed in their sins."

The crowd buzzed over Enoch's words. This was to be a showdown between Cain and Enoch, not between God and the crowd. The crowd wanted to be spectators, not participants. They had not counted on being dragged into the contest.

Many men and women and boys and girls trembled as the prophet of God continued: "Again, I say to each one of you in the temple and surrounding the temple -- Depart from evil. Draw nigh unto God, and He will draw nigh unto you."

Enoch's words made everyone uncomfortable in and near the temple. Some people, fearful of what Enoch's God might do, began to shove and push their children away from the temple, away from the tables of free food surrounding the temple. But most people, although a touch uneasy, figured that Enoch's God was no more powerful than Zaava's god.

The priestly guards around the temple all held their positions. They, too, were a bit uneasy; but they were too well trained and too fearful of Cain to be moved by the threat of a mere shepherd. Yet, more than one of the guards had fresh memories of Theron and his squad and of the day that the Sheep Man preached from atop the Tower in the City of Cain. What new tricks might this peculiar Sheep Man pull out of his bag today?

The three people inside the temple all reacted differently to the ominous threat from the prophet of God. Lalomar, emboldened by his new position of authority as priest of the Temple of Gom, turned toward Aram and threatened: "If your brother does any harm to my temple, I will kill him and all of his family."

Aram was stunned. He had never counted the cost of his active role as a builder of, then priest of, the Temple of Gom. The young man broke out into a cold sweat from the two threats hurled just now. Aram knew his brother was sincere; now, he just wished that his brother was sincerely wrong. Somehow, Aram hoped, this stupid showdown could end with no one, not even his brother, injured.

Adah was in more turmoil than even Aram. Enoch's words brought renewed hope in her heart as she took her mind off of her earthly father and raised her gaze to heavenly heights. "Oh, God in Heaven," she wondered aloud, "will You really forgive me after all of the terrible sins I have committed? Will You really forgive me after how much I have hurt my father? Will You really forgive me for the death of my baby?" Tears streamed down her cheeks as she spoke aloud one final time:

"Oh, God, if I draw near unto You, will You really draw near unto me?"

Adah dropped her gaze down to her feet. She tried to take a step forward. Much to her amazement, and to the amazement of Lalomar and Aram, her foot actually moved. She tried to take another step forward. That foot moved likewise.

A spirit of peace began to creep into Adah's heart with each step, shoving aside the spirit of fear that had ruled in her heart for so long. As she took another step, then another and another, the spirit of peace increased and the spirit of fear decreased.

Within a moment or two, Adah reached the cordon of guards surrounding the temple, pushing her way past the startled guardians of the temple. As she pushed pass Zaava's servants who had been serving roast cow, Adah could hear the entreating voice of Aram: "Come back, Adah! Come back!"

But there was no turning back for Adah now. With each step away from the temple, away from her degradation, Enoch's words rang louder and louder in her mind: "Depart from evil!" Faster and faster she ran, pushing her way through the crowd, crying aloud, uncaring of any man's response: "Father, will You really forgive me?"

Finally, she broke free from the crowd. "Enoch! Enoch!" she cried to the prophet of God on the platform above.

"Adah!" Enoch cried. The prophet of God ran to the steps, flew down from the platform, and raced to the approaching young lady.

Adah flew into Enoch's arms. "Enoch, O Enoch," she wept as Enoch led her back to the east platform: "Will God really forgive me?"

Enoch wept also. "God certainly will, Adah. He has been waiting for you for a long time." Enoch walked the searching penitent up the steps of the east platform and handed her over to Perna. "Perna, please take a minute to hug Adah, then tell her how she can know for certain that God will forgive her of all of her sins."

As Perna welcomed Adah as her own daughter, Enoch turned and once again, for the final time, faced the Temple of Gom.

## Chapter Forty-seven

# The Judgment of God

With renewed hope in the power of God, Enoch faced the expectant, anxious crowd. "Hereby ye shall know that the Lord, the One True God, hath sent me to do all these works; for I have not done them of mine own hand." The crowd, moved by the scene of the young priestess departing from the temple and racing to Enoch, truly wondered if perhaps Enoch's God did have more power than the senseless Great Ebony Cow.

The mood of the crowd changed suddenly as Enoch spoke his next words. "If the Lord makes a new thing, and the earth opens her mouth and swallows the temple, with all of the guards and all of the food tables surrounding it, and they go down quick into the pit, then ye shall understand that Cain and Zaava have provoked the Lord."

Before anyone inside or outside the temple could move, a great trembling shook the earth. Lalomar, Aram, the guards, Zaava's servants, even Cain himself, became rattled. Cain turned to Zaava and asked: "Can Enoch pull this thing off?"

"Not without his magic staff," Zaava quickly responded.

But, as if he had heard Zaava's words spoken from the west platform, Enoch continued to prophesy: "I do not need the staff of God to call upon God and His almighty power. The power is not in me, nor in my staff, but in God Himself." Then, with a terrible finality, Enoch boomed across the marketplace: "My God is a consuming fire!"

Immediately, the ground began to rumble again. Every eye in the marketplace looked down with terror as the earth began to move up and down as waves on the sea. Then, as suddenly as they started, the earth waves stopped. Every heart was pounding when suddenly a tremendous, deafening boom filled the air. Before anyone could scream, the earth surrounding the temple began to crack and split and divide.

The crack in the earth started in front of the temple directly under one of the food tables, then followed the path of the food tables around the temple until the temple was completely surrounded. The crowd was frozen in terror at this new thing. Before anyone could move, a great flame of consuming fire shot upward through the crack to a height of forty feet, encircling the temple and instantly consuming, as if it were an evening sacrifice, the tables of roast cow. All of Zaava's servants attending to the tables were also instantly consumed, as were many city dwellers unfortunate to have not earlier moved away from the food tables.

The crowd in the marketplace panicked. The awful flame and awful stench of death drove everyone outside the temple to flee madly from the scene of destruction. He who hesitated was soon trampled under foot by the crazed crowd.

Inside the ring of fire stood Cain's terrified guards, unnerved by the earth waves, the sudden sheet of fire, and the hysterical crowd fleeing the temple. Yet, still more fearful of Cain, they continued to hold their position as the temperature inside the temple continued to rise.

On the east platform, Adah clung tightly to Perna as she watched the awful devastation at the place where she had stood only minutes before. Enoch's eyes were focused upon his brother, trapped inside the flaming ring of fire. Aram's eyes, wild with fear, darted back and forth searching hopelessly for some escape.

But Aram was helpless as God's judgment continued to pour upon the Temple of Gom. As the flame roared through the evening sky, another incredible boom shook the air. Then, the ground inside the ring of fire began to sink.

The guards finally lost their composure. First one, then another, then all hundred guards flung down their shields and spears in mad panic and began to run in all directions to escape the doomed temple. But there was nowhere to run. There was no escape. When a few of the guards tried to run through the ring of fire, they were instantly consumed.

Cries of sheer terror filled the evening sky as the temple began to sink lower and lower into the earth. The pillars of the temple began to crack, then topple. As Enoch watched in horror, a falling pillar crushed his younger brother to death. Lower and lower the doomed temple sank.

Then, with one final mighty boom, the wall of flame ceased to shoot into the sky. With an awful gulp, the earth swallowed the ruins of the Temple of Gom. The guards, Lalomar, Aram, and the Temple of Gom were seen no more.

## Chapter Forty-eight

# "Let's Go Home"

Ludim watched the scene of destruction as smoke continued to ascend into the evening sky. He watched as a large man, whom he quickly identified as his son, dashed up the steps of the west platform and attempted to console his wife, who was sobbing hysterically. As he looked over the scene again, the blacksmith observed: "The Lord has spoken."

Ludim's words seemed to lift the pall of silence that had engulfed the east platform. Arphaxad turned to his friend and shouted: "We won, Enoch! We won!"

But Enoch was not rejoicing. His shoulders were slumped, his eyes downcast. He could only reply: "I have lost my brother."

Arphaxad immediately toned down his enthusiasm as he also noticed that Ludim was solemn and Adah seemed to be in shock. The solemnity and quietude on the east platform was short-lived, however, as a shrieking voice started from the west platform and moved toward the east platform. "I'll kill you! I'll kill you!"

Arphaxad turned and saw his sister running past the south gate toward the steps of the east platform. "I'll kill you! I'll kill you!" Zaava shrieked again.

Enoch, still consumed with grief over his fallen brother, did not even hear the shrill threats of the high priestess of the former Temple of Gom. As Zaava bounded up the steps, Ludim and Arphaxad quickly dashed to intercept her. She thrashed as her brother and father-in-law restrained her. "I'll kill you! I'll kill you!" she repeated over and over again until she slumped to the ground, overcome with disappointment and tears. All of her dreams, all of her ambitions, had just gone up in smoke and disappeared.

From the west platform, Cain and Tubal looked at the pitiful Zaava collapsed on the other platform. "She tends to get hysterical when things don't go her way," Tubal dryly explained.

"Yes," Cain agreed, "but God did make women more emotional than we men."

"So, you do believe in Enoch's God?" Tubal asked with some surprise.

"Of course, I do, dear Tubal," Cain replied, "but not in the same way that Enoch believes. I do believe that his God exists, for I have spoken to Him, a long time ago. But I have ignored Enoch's God for hundreds of years. Now, I do things my own way."

Tubal looked upon his benefactor with some bemusement. "But it appears that Enoch's God did not ignore Cain today."

Cain looked disdainfully upon the clever Tubal. "My dear Tubal, I do not fear Enoch's God. Sure, Enoch's God can do many, many things -- cause earthquakes, burn up people with fire -- but there is one thing Enoch's God cannot do."

Tubal asked curiously: "What one thing is that, Cain?"

"Enoch's God cannot kill Cain!" he said boldly. "I am invincible! I am immortal!"

Tubal could not restrain a laugh. "That's ridiculous, Cain. All men must die."

"All men but I!" Cain replied forcefully. "God is afraid to kill me. He could have killed me long ago when I killed my brother Abel. He could have killed me today, along with Zaava's servants, my guards, Lalomar, and Aram. But God didn't and can't. I am immortal, Tubal. I shall never die."

Meanwhile, after the crowd finally dispersed in the marketplace and a few stragglers were going through the litter, the people on the east platform finally readied to leave. Ludim and Perna bade farewell to their friends and returned home to check on Martha. Arphaxad led the grieving Enoch and the subdued Adah down the steps of the east platform. Arphaxad paused to pick up Enoch's staff as they walked through the south gate.

They found Elam's horse and wagon right where they had been left earlier that day. Arphaxad checked the horse over to make sure that he was none the worse from the mad dash to the City of Gom. Arphaxad was satisfied that the horse could haul the wagon and three passengers home, so he gently assisted Adah and Enoch into the wagon, letting Adah get some sleep in the back.

The ride home was mostly filled with silence. Adah slept soundly as her body started to recover from the many tragic events of the last couple of days. Enoch's thoughts were upon Aram and Jared. "What will I say to my father?" Enoch kept asking himself over and over and over. Arphaxad just carefully steered the horse, and thought over and over again of God's great judgment and triumph at the City of Gom.

As they neared Elam's house, Adah finally woke up. "Where are we, Enoch?" she gently asked as she rubbed sleep out of her eyes.

Enoch was awakened out of his silent requiem. "We are almost home, dear Adah," Enoch gently replied.

"Your home, Enoch?" Adah hesitantly asked.

"No, your home, Adah," Enoch replied.

Arphaxad and Enoch could hear sobs behind them. Then they heard Adah ask another sincere question: "Enoch, do you think that my daddy will receive me home?"

Enoch was not sure how to respond. Finally, he asked Adah if she would mind sitting up front on the seat with the two men. Arphaxad slowed down the horse as young Adah maneuvered herself between the two big men on the front seat. Enoch put his arm around the doubting Adah, and assured her: "I am fully confident that Elam will welcome you back home, Adah. Your father loves you very much."

Adah sobbed some more. "But I have hurt my daddy so much, Enoch. How could he ever forgive me?"

His thoughts turned briefly to his own daughter Crista, long lost but not forgotten. How Enoch would love to receive his little Crista home tonight. Then Enoch replied: "Your heavenly Father has forgiven you tonight, Adah. Your earthly father will, too."

Adah cried again as she thought of the great peace that had flooded her soul that night as she had asked God to forgive her of all her sins and as she trusted in the coming Redeemer as her Savior. But her new faith was in God. She did not yet have the faith to trust in Elam to forgive her. Between sobs, she confessed to the prophet of God: "But I am not bringing home my daddy's granddaughter," Adah wept bitterly. "Daddy will never forgive me for that."

Enoch wished he could wipe away all of Adah's fears and all of Adah's tears. All he could say was: "Adah, your father fought to bring you home just yesterday. He will surely welcome you home tonight, with open arms."

As the young girl continued to sob, Arphaxad drove the wagon to the top of the hill overlooking Elam's farm. The horse neighed as its nose caught the familiar scents of home. Arphaxad could make out the shape of a man standing in the lit doorway of Elam's home, looking up to the top of the hill.

The moon was full that night, just above the horizon at the top of the hill overlooking the farm. The three figures in the wagon were silhouetted against the full moon for just a fleeting moment. Suddenly, the night air was interrupted again by the glorious shout from the watchful man in the doorway: "Adah!"

Elam rushed out of his house and began to run up the hill. The sound of his voice was the only sound of hope that Adah needed to hear. She stood up and cried out: "Daddy!" As she scrambled out of the wagon and ran down the hill to her father, the doubts and fears of many years evaporated in the cool night air.

Enoch and Arphaxad sat quietly, watching the joyful reunion of the prodigal daughter and her longsuffering father. Then both men climbed down from the wagon. Enoch took the reins, tied them to a nearby tree, and started walking back down the road. "Let's go home, my friend. Let's go home."

# Acknowledgements

When the Hamilton family went through the great tragedy of 1998, we discovered that God's grace is sufficient for the greatest trials. God comforted us in three major ways: through God's Word, through God's music, and through God's people. A special thanks goes to all of the friends and family who supported us in our time of desperate need.

My family continues to be avid supporters of ***The Methuselah Chronicles.***

* My faithful wife Jan continues to help with the ministry as she proofs my books.

* My daughter Joy married Casey King in 1999 and moved to Wisconsin. Since then, Joy and Casey have joined the staff of Glory to Glory Ministries.

* My son Daniel married Jessica Acierno in 2001 and moved to Kent, Ohio, where he is continuing his studies to become a lawyer.

My pastor, Pastor John Jones, continues to be a big supporter of all of my writing projects. It means so much when my pastor is such an active supporter.

Just as with ***Methuselah's Father***, ***The First Prophet*** was edited by Mary Storm. Mary puts her heart (and spills her blood, i.e. her red pen) all over my manuscripts.

Probably my biggest fan on Earth was my daughter Glory. She loved my books. She wanted to be a Christian writer herself. Glory read and loved the draft version of ***The First Prophet***, but because of her seemingly untimely death in 1998, she was not able to read this published version. God has used the years since 1998 to comfort us, to heal us, and to raise up Glory to Glory Ministries. ***The First Prophet*** is published under that new publisher and is dedicated to Glory's memory.

# *Coming soon . . .*

**Book Three of**
**The Methuselah Chronicles**

# The Final Journey

**by Terry Lee Hamilton**

Enoch's love for his Redeemer and for his fellow man lead him to pursue his God-ordained prophetic ministry over the course of hundreds of years, facing triumph and tragedy in both his family and ministry.

***The Final Journey*** inevitably leads Enoch to his final showdown with Cain, a never-forgotten moment in which the forces of good prevail over the forces of evil.

But before Enoch leaves this world, in an unforgettable scene of compassion, God makes good on His precious promise that Enoch will be reunited with his long-lost daughter Crista.

If you liked the characters and action and suspense of ***Methuselah's Father*** and ***The First Prophet,*** you will love ***The Final Journey***.

Order each book in ***The Methuselah Chronicles*** series of historical novels by writing Glory to Glory Ministries, 1813 E. 45th St., Ashtabula, OH 44004 or e-mailing to hamiltonfamily@alltel.net. God bless you!